CHRISTMAS BIZARRE

A SUMMIT SPRINGS NOVEL

JODI PAYNE

BA TORTUGA

Christmas Bizarre
Copyright © 2022 by Jodi Payne & BA Tortuga

Cover illustration by AJ Corza
http://www.seeingstatic.com/
Cover content is for illustrative purposes only and any person depicted on the cover is a model.

ISBN: 978-1-951011-86-4

Published by Tygerseye Publishing, LLC
December 2022
Printed in the USA

To our wives.
Merry Christmas!

1

I've got this. I've totally got this.

"What the—"

Charlotte Miller frowned at the dashboard of her rented mid-size sedan and wondered what the hell she was thinking. The drive from Denver to her hometown of Summit Springs shouldn't take more than ninety minutes, maybe two hours if she stopped at the Sunset Diner before she hit the mountain pass, but she'd been on the road that long already.

She should have gotten the hint when she discovered the diner was closed. Not only did she leave hungry, but she left stupid too, without checking the weather to see if the snow got worse up the hill.

The snow always got worse up the hill.

It was barely a week after Thanksgiving, and she should have known better. This pass didn't usually close, but it could be a hairy drive in bad weather. She should have paid the extra money to rent something with four-wheel drive. Or waited two days. Or have been better at her job so she didn't need to escape Denver under cover of a family emergency.

A few more snowflakes, and *she* would be the family emergency. Wouldn't that be completely in character?

"What? Shit. No. Wait..." The orange idiot light blinking on the dashboard was a "check engine" warning. Check engine? Okay fine, so she didn't get the four-wheel drive, but the car wasn't a total POS. She was cheap but not *that* cheap. Was this a joke? She was about to crest the mountain in a near-blizzard, but instead of sliding off the road into snowy oblivion—as one did—she was going to break down instead?

She kept her foot on the gas, begging the gods of ugly four-door sedans to be kind. "Fuck. Don't you die on me, you little fucker. Um. Please-thanks?"

Charlotte was not going to cry. Not at all. She was sophisticated. Suave. Not single because her fiancée had dumped her for some pediatrician in Seattle. Not in huge trouble at work because she'd called the marketing director of their biggest client a bigot. She totally had this.

Fuck her life.

For a second it seemed like it was going to be okay. The light stayed on, but the car was moving along. It even seemed like the snow might be letting up. She took a breath and puffed it out, willing her shoulders to relax.

And then the second was gone.

The engine sputtered and made this horrible noise. It felt like the car bucked underneath her and then it was over. She rolled to a stop with a dead engine.

Goddamn it.

"Goddamn it!" she shouted, pounding on the steering wheel. When she tried to turn the engine over again the car made an evil screeching sound as if Satan himself were in there playing the electric guitar.

So, fuck yeah. She lost it.

"Fuck you, you stupid piece-of-shit-grandpa-mobile!" She pounded on the steering wheel, the window, the dashboard. "Fuck you!"

Then the tears did come—those fucking tears that she'd held at bay since yesterday morning when her twin brother had called.

"Lottie, I fell off the barn and broke my arm."

"Lottie, Dad had a heart attack and he's in Grand Junction."

"Lottie, Gram and Aunt Deenie aren't capable of pulling off the Summit Springs Bazaar."

"Lottie, I need you. We're going to lose the farm."

That last sentence had been the straw that broke her knock-off Louboutins.

She would do anything for Jacob, and together, they'd burn the world down for the family farm. But first she had to get off this fucking road and not freeze her tits off. They were perky and she was proud of them. Rosalie had even said how much she'd miss them before she'd taken back her diamond ring and walked out the door.

Bitch.

She took a deep breath and tried to calm down. She shouldn't waste all that hydration on tears if she was going to be stuck here, right? Did it even work like that? Whatever, her drama llama act wasn't helping. She swiped at her eyes, then tried the engine again, but Satan must have won out because the fucking thing was silent. Dead and silent.

Fine. No problem. She had a cell phone.

But who to call? Aunt Deenie was adorable but useless in an emergency, Jacob was, oh god...probably in a big cast or something. She should have asked him about that, huh? *Hm.* And she was still in denial about Dad, period. He was going to be fine. Just fine.

Fine, damn it.

So, who did that leave? AAA? The police? Mountain rescue? *Oh!* Maybe Gerry March was still on that team. Gerry was butchy-beautiful and being rescued by her would make all of this so worth it.

She pulled out her phone, beaming at the light pouring, all her favorite apps reminding her why she loved Denver. Summit Springs didn't even have a big box store. She needed Target and...

Why the hell wasn't her Safari working?

Maybe because it's a fucking snowstorm, and you have no bars, idiot.

Charlotte hated that goddamn voice—the one that talked to her like she was a moron. Talked to herself. Whatever. The ugly one that convinced her she was the reason her almost-marriage didn't happen, and that she couldn't do that job she was about to get fired from anyway. The one that was telling her that she should have rented a four-wheel-drive car. The one that was right about having no bars.

"Fuck this." No more tears. That was for people who wanted to deal with their shit. She wanted to bury hers in a deep, deep fucking hole. She put on her hazards—that was something anyway—and got out of the car.

Jesus, it was cold, and windy, and this was like January bullshit weather not the first week of December. What the hell? At least she had the right coat on and a pair of boots. She never got to wear these fuzzy ones in Denver, and she was happy to be in them now.

She opened the trunk, ducking under the hatch for cover, and pulled out a bottle of red wine.

She wasn't driving. She wasn't even walking in this crap; she'd freeze. Nope. She was going to drink.

Assuming she had a corkscrew in the glove compartment, of course.

2

"Come on, you beautiful assholes! Mush!" Naomi "Lars" Beckett's laugh rang through the spruce and fir, her sled flying over the snow. "Take us home, girls."

Misty and Bianca barked loud, the lead pair driving the eight-dog team with the sheer confidence of three years of being in charge. Good thing too, because Lars hadn't expected the storm to hit this fast, or this hard. It was supposed to arrive in the early hours tomorrow, not the late afternoon today.

Still, she knew this part of the tree farm like the back of her hand, and if she needed to stop, she had Pappy's hunting lodge midway. No worries.

At least she thought she knew it. She didn't remember flashing lights. What was going on up by the road? Was that a new signal or something? She liked to keep her distance from the road because the snow up by the mountain pass got squirrely after it was plowed, but no one would be plowing yet. Even road services were caught off-guard by this storm.

She could ignore it.

She ought to ignore it.

Oh shit, who was she kidding? She'd never ignored a single thing in her entire goddamn life. She was the queen of curiosity.

"Gee! Gee!"

Misty and Bianca turned right, the swing dogs following them without a hint of hesitation. That brought her closer to the lights, and as the team drew her alongside the road, she saw it was a piece of shit sedan.

It wasn't stuck in the snowbank. The tires looked fine. It seemed like whoever it was had just pulled off the road, and by the clearly fogged-up windows, they were probably still inside.

"Whoa! Whoa, guys!" Her team loved to go, and they weren't happy at all with stopping, but they managed, sort of.

She was only going to have to walk back about a car length.

"Stand, guys. I'll be right back." She set the snow hook before trekking back. She had to know who was out here on the mountain. Someone had to have taken the wrong exit.

She trudged through the snow, eyes squinting into the wind, and she knocked on the driver's side door. A second later the door opened, ice cracking around the hinges and snow falling from the roof. And did she smell a cabernet?

"Oh, hey!" Big blue eyes blinked at her from a pretty face framed with messy, dark hair, and she got a confused-looking smile. "You're not the police. Are you real? I've had like half a bottle of wine."

"I am not police. I am real. And I can tell a little. Are you okay?" Do you know that you're adorable? Because damn.

"Well, I'm in a crappy rental broken down in the snow, and I've been sitting here an hour or so. I'm okay, I guess, but I have *got* to pee." The woman was dead serious. There was no irony in that statement at all. "Also, it would be nice to...be somewhere warmer. Do you have a truck?"

"Yeah, but not here." Still, Lars couldn't just leave this girl out here—not if she'd been drinking. Hell, not under any circumstance. "Are you wearing good boots?"

The pretty face lit up. "Yes! I was so excited to be coming here, I wore my Malvellas. Are they not the cutest? I don't usually pay full price for anything, but these are warm and waterproof too."

"Good deal. Let's get you all bundled up, and we'll get you out of here." The woman was only a little thing—Lars would put her on the sled and run behind.

"Yeah? Thanks. Should I bring the wine? Probably not, huh? Yeah, okay that was weird. Sorry, I've had a day. Wine was a better option than a nervous breakdown. I'm Charlotte, by the way." Charlotte climbed out of the car, and Lars was pleased to see she had on a nice warm coat with a hood to go along with her fancy boots. "Fuck, it's cold."

"Wine is a fine idea, but we have to get moving. This storm is bad." And it wasn't letting up. She was about an hour away from the house in clear weather, but this wasn't anywhere near that.

Charlotte leaned against her and looked around as they started walking. "So...where did you say your truck was?"

"It's at home, honey. I was out with the dogs." She pointed to the dogsled, the team of eight wagging Huskies.

"What is that? Is that sled?" Charlotte stared at her from under her fur-lined hood, grinning. "No way. I'm being rescued by a dogsledder? Seriously?"

"That's me. I'm going to get you up on the sled, and I need you to hold on. I'll run along behind."

"Really? Oh, this day just got so much better." Charlotte

eagerly followed her instructions to the letter, standing just the way she was told and holding on.

Lord save her from drunk tourists. Still, Charlotte was a pretty one, and she smelled like wine and strawberries.

"Ready!" Lars bellowed, and Chuck bit Moose's butt, waking the lazy pup up. One day Moose would take Chuck's job as a wheel, but that wasn't going to be today.

Her team straightened up in their harnesses, ears and tails up, all ready to go. "Hold on, now. Alright!"

Misty and Bianca headed off with a jerk, and she started running.

"Whoo!" Charlotte laughed as they took off and had to be less drunk than she seemed because she held on tight and kept her balance. "Oh my god. This is so cool!"

Cool? More like bitter. Lars wrapped her scarf around her mouth and nose, and that air was pushing in her lungs like ice. The dogs pushed through the snow, and Lars fought to run in the tracks they left, but it wasn't twenty minutes before her legs felt leaden.

Charlotte had gone quiet too, still holding on, but crouched a bit and hiding in her hood.

Dammit. She checked her bearings, the compass. Okay, she was ten minutes from the hunting shed, tops, and possibly another hour from home. A person could freeze to death in forty-five minutes. "Haw! Haw!"

The team took a sharp left and moved into the trees.

"Mush! Mush!"

"Whoa." Charlotte ducked as the branches flew by. "That woke me up!"

"We're going to the hunting shack!" She screamed to be heard over the wind.

"Tell me we can make a fire!" Charlotte shouted back.

"There's emergency supplies!" She had the standard

emergency stuff on the sled—food for the dogs, sleeping bag, fuel and stove, and a handful of granola bars. Pappy's shack would have dry rations, wood, and water.

"Great! This seems like an emergency!" Charlotte ducked unnecessarily. "This is kind of crazy!"

"No shit on that." This was epic, and she had to get her product out, make sure that the tree lot was stocked, and the high school kids were there to help load and pour cocoa and...

"Whoa!" The team damn near shot right past the cabin. "Whoa, team!"

Charlotte leaned back hard as the team came to a fast halt and landed in her arms. "Wow. *Wow*. My feet are frozen, and I can't feel my face but...wow."

"Yeah. I hear you." Lord love a duck, Charlotte was about as pretty as a picture.

Charlotte didn't move, just hung there in her arms a minute and looked at her with watery blue eyes. "What's your name?"

"Lars. Lars Beckett. Come on, honey, let's get you inside so I can unhook the dogs." They'd do their business while she got a fire going and got everyone fed and settled for the night. Between the fire, the blankets, the sleeping bag, and the dogs, they'd be fine.

"Oh, sure. What can I do to help?"

She steered Charlotte inside and closed the door against the wind.

"Oh, that's better." Charlotte lowered her hood, then cupped her hands and blew on her fingers. She was shivering pretty hard. "Mittens would have been a good idea, huh?"

"Yeah. Let me unhook the dogs. You know how to start a

fire, by any chance?" That would help things move a hell of a lot faster.

"Uh, yeah. Yeah. It's been a while but...yes. I can." Charlotte shook her hands out. "Wood. Wood Stove. Got it."

"Matches are in the matchbox. Wood is in that little door. I'll be right back in with supplies and dogs."

"Got it. But uh...hey. Lars?" Charlotte smiled at her, warming her even without a fire. "Thank you."

"I'm glad we ran across you. This is bound to be warmer than that car." And way more interesting than sleeping alone tonight.

3

Charlotte had never felt so cold in her entire life. Once the fire was lit, she kicked off her boots and shrugged out of her coat, both of which were so wet they were making her feel even colder. She poked around and found a blanket in a chest near the door and sat down cross-legged on the brick in front of the wood stove to thaw out.

She was pretty stoked that she'd managed to get the fire going, and it was starting to really take off. She'd grown up with a wood stove, so stacking the logs and lighting the kindling was still in her muscle memory. God, it was nice to not have to think too hard about something for once. With her luck she'd burn the cabin down around them, but for the moment it was all good. Easy. Familiar. She actually felt useful.

Of course she'd broken two fingernails trying not to drop a log on her foot. All she could do was sigh as she frowned at her hand. Par for the course. Broken fingernails to go along with a broken car, a broken career, and a broken heart. She had a long list of things in her life that were broken right now. What was one more? It was a good thing she was too cheap for a real manicure. She was wearing her favorite iridescent powder blue polish though, so there was that.

And there was also Lars, who'd rescued her on a dogsled. There was so much awesome in that statement she didn't even know where to begin. Dogsled. Rescue. A woman named "Lars." Lars looked pretty athletic and had gorgeous eyes too, but that was about all she could see because the dogsledder had been bundled up tight.

No one was ever going to believe that some stud in a bright yellow snowsuit had scooped her up and brought her to a cabin. Maybe she should get pictures. Proof so she could tell stories.

But stories to who? Her brother? Mom? Her best friend, Fern?

Or maybe this should be one of those things she kept to herself. Fern wasn't in town so that would be easy. Keeping it from Jacob might be a trick, but it wouldn't be the first time he let her get away with trying. She could decide all that once she got a second to talk with whoever was really under the yellow jumpsuit, right?

She jumped when Lars came lumbering in with a handful of stuff. "I fed the dogs. I'll melt some snow for them to drink and then let them in to sleep."

"Sure. Cool." Seriously? She was going to sleep in a remote cabin with a bunch of sled dogs. It was getting so no one would believe this story anyway. "I bet they're pretty once the snow melts. The fire is...trying."

Lars peered at it quickly. "Give it some more air, and it'll perk up."

She rolled her eyes at herself and reached for the flue.

Right. Air. Just when she was starting to feel useful. Why she thought she could waltz in and run the annual bazaar she didn't know. But she didn't have a choice, did she?

By the time Lars came in with eight of the biggest dogs she'd ever seen, the fire was blazing, the room seemed almost cozy.

"Oh my god." She popped up, moving so they could get closer to the fire. "Come on you guys...come sit, dry off. Wow. They didn't look this big from the sled."

"I know. They're my puppies." Lars started stripping down, revealing a tall strawberry blonde with bright brown eyes, freckles scattered across her cheeks.

Oh.

She was such a sucker for freckles.

"I hate to break it to you, but these look more like full-grown dogs." She grinned, trying to be...playful? Okay, fine, she was flirting. It took her exactly thirty seconds to get there. Why not? If Lars wasn't interested, she'd know soon enough. And if she was, it wasn't like Charlotte would see this woman again.

"Yeah, but they're my poopsie-poos." Lars laughed, the sound deep and wonderful and sexual as fuck as she began to strip off her bright yellow outwear and boots.

She dropped the blanket on a bench, keeping her eyes on Lars. "They're kind of a stinky bunch though."

"Yep. You hooligans settle in. She'll love on everyone in a minute." Lars put her hand out flat, then moved it down.

To her utter shock, all eight dogs plopped onto the floor.

She blinked, astonished at how well trained they were. "That was like magic."

"They're a great pack. I love them. I have another six at home."

"Yeah? Is someone staying with them? Are they okay?"

She took a couple of steps closer to Lars, those shiny brown eyes pulling her in like a magnet. "I don't know about you, but I couldn't get cell service on the road. I thought I was going to freeze to death out there."

"They are built for this weather. I fed them this morning, and they're in the barn. These guys have worked hard." Lars pulled her in, hands rubbing her upper arms, warming her up. "Are you just driving through, honey?"

Oh, that felt good. Lars had strong, warm hands and, now that they were closer, Charlotte could really admire all the freckles. But did they have to talk? Did she want to answer questions? "I have business in Summit Springs. This is going to make an incredible story."

"Yeah? Never been rescued by a dogsled before?" Lars's eyes were so clear, so pretty.

"Never been rescued by a—gorgeous—dogsledder before."

"Gorgeous?" That little chuckle was wry, and the rubbing got slower, so steady and hypnotic. "Thank you, sweetheart. That's a hell of a compliment coming from you."

"From me? God, I hate to think what I look like right now." But the praise somehow sat just right with her, and the deliberate touch was everything.

"Like you've been on an amazing ride with a wild woman." That wink liked to burn her to the ground with pure naughtiness.

"Oh yeah? Are you wild?" She bit her lip as she grinned at Lars, matching that naughty look.

"I am. One of those mountain woman you hear about." Lars chuckled and rubbed one finger along her bottom lip.

"The ones that eat people?" she teased, reaching for Lars's wrist and kissing her palm.

"Mmhmm..." That sound was pure growl, and it made Charlotte's toes curl. "Nom nom nom, pretty bird."

Oh, what the hell. It had been a shitty month and a shitty day, and then it became this amazing, fantasy rescue. The Universe had to be telling her to seize the moment. Or the dogsledder. Whatever.

Had to.

She went up on her toes and tried, but she was just a half an inch too short and that made her giggle. She leaned into Lars so she didn't lose her balance. "C'mere."

Lars cupped the back of her head and leaned down, holding her gaze as those surprisingly soft lips pressed against hers, letting her decide how deep the kiss went.

Sweet. Unnecessary, but sweet.

She basked in it, trying not to think about the fiancée that had just walked out of her life, who had never given her a moment like this. Not that she needed it; she'd tried to kiss Lars first after all. It was just...kind. She pushed everything that was snowy dogsled related out of her mind and opened her lips to let Lars in.

Apparently, it was all Lars needed, because she bent down, tugging her close, and that tongue pushed in between her lips, tasting her like she was sweeter than honey.

Oh, yes please. The only thing better than a hot dogsledder was a hot dogsledder who was into women. This really was a fantasy, and she was going to enjoy every second of it. She slid her tongue along Lars's and arched in hard, then pushed a hand into that unruly hair. It was softer than she'd expected, and she played through it, fingers making their way to Lars's nape.

The kisses blended, one into another, and it was wild and hot, and they ended up on the old sofa, like both their sets of knees gave out at the same time.

She wasn't cold anymore. Not a bit. She wanted this woman, and she didn't question it. "This is cool. I'm good. Are you good?" She hoped so, because her fingers wanted more of Lars's skin, and she couldn't deny the delicious ache between her thighs.

"We're not going anywhere 'til the morning. Why not?" Lars cupped one of her breasts, thumb rubbing her nipple through bra and sweater firmly enough to draw it to a firm peak. "Oh, isn't that pretty. Let me see?"

That touch felt good. That was the touch of someone who knew what they wanted, and it was good to be wanted. She smiled and sat back a bit, then tugged her cable-knit sweater off over her head. She hadn't worn one of her pretty bras; in fact she wasn't sure she'd packed any of those in what was likely her frozen suitcase. This one was just simple, not that it mattered because she wasn't keeping it on anyway. She reached back to unhook it, and let it slide off her shoulders as seductively as possible.

"Mmm..." Damn, Lars stared at her like she was a bar of chocolate. Then she swooped down and leaned Charlotte back in the same motion, lips wrapping around one of her nipples, surrounding it in pure fire.

"Oh..." She didn't hold back her moan, shifting to stretch out under Lars and reaching down to tug at the heavy sweater Lars was wearing.

She pulled it off, coming face-to-face with wild color— Lars's back and arms were covered with tattoos. Every single inch a riot of flowers, like she was a bouquet.

"Oh my god. You're...blooming. You're a garden." It was beautiful work, and she felt like she'd been let in on a secret. "Your ink."

Lars lifted her face, and her lips were already red, a little swollen from her suction. "And you're lush. You smell like heaven."

"Yeah? You like the scent of wine and frantic desperation, huh?" She slid her hands down Lars's back as far as she could reach, just managing to get her fingers under the waistband of Lars's pants, finding thermals under there.

Lars winked at her. "Layers. That's the secret."

Then Lars caught her neglected nipple, fingers dancing over her waist.

She shivered and her abs jumped at the light touch. "Secret...to what? Chastity?" She fumbled and pushed at all the fabric, distracted by Lars's quick tongue. "Oh, god."

Lars teased her, giving her a hint of teeth, just stealing her breath with a zing, the sensation shooting right down her belly. Two could play that teasing game so she drew the fingernails she had left down Lars's back from her shoulders all the way to those maddening layers, then gave the waistband of the thermals a snap.

"Oh ho!" Lars dropped a sucking kiss to the tip of her nipple, then began to lick and nibble all the way down her belly, before heading north again to plunder her mouth.

Fuck yes. She let Lars drive the kiss, bending and twisting at the whim of that insistent tongue. She hooked her heel around one long thigh and touched their hips tightly together, rocking into all of Lars's strength.

She wanted to make it perfectly clear that she was into this, that she wanted to have a wild night, to take advantage of this...gift.

Lars seemed to hear her, and she cupped her ass, dragging them together, humping down against her.

"Yes!" The couch made an ominous noise and that seemed just right somehow, both of them groaning under

Lars's perfect weight. She was burning up, needing. "Please, yes."

Lars shifted, one thigh sliding up between her legs, the pressure just right, her clit getting just enough friction to send her higher.

She gasped, eyes locking onto Lars's as they rocked together, everything building just right. "There...just like that. Fuck yes." Just exactly right.

"So goddamn pretty." Lars watched her like a hawk, then color flooded her cheeks.

God, this woman. So strong and capable, but in this moment just as fragile as she was. "Good, baby?" She rocked again, stars twinkling at the edge of her vision. "Just a...so close, oh fuck..."

"Yeah..." Lars kissed her so hard it stole her breath, and all she could do was tumble over the edge along with Lars.

"Damn," she whispered once she could breathe again, she and helped Lars settle on the narrow couch beside her. Her limbs felt heavy, like she'd—like she'd what? Ridden a dogsled through a blizzard? She started to laugh softly, as she snuggled against Lars.

"I know. I hear you. How often do you pick up a gorgeous woman in the snow?"

"Or get laid by a hot dogsledder in a cabin surrounded by her eight wet dogs." She kissed Lars quickly. She wasn't ready for this crazy fantasy to be over. "Your tongue is magic by the way."

Lars winked at her. "Remember that for next time."

Like there would be a next time.

That was the whole point. No next time. A random night with a random woman she'd never see again. It's not like she was going to be up here in the woods ever. No, even on the farm she had a big comfy bed in her big comfy room that had electricity, heat, and hot water. Jacob had a couple of basset hounds but she could just imagine the look he'd get if he asked them to pull a dogsled.

She chuckled softly and snuggled in. Like Lars said, they couldn't go anywhere until the morning.

4

Thank god for instant oatmeal. It wasn't the greatest thing in the world, but it worked, and that was all they needed.

Lars had enjoyed the hell out of Ms. Sexy, but she knew that hot bodies in the middle of a snowstorm was a romance novel thing, and she wasn't romance novel type. So oatmeal and instant coffee, then...what? To the house? To the car?

"I guess I need a tow truck, huh?" Charlotte winced as she sipped the coffee. "Oh. Strong."

"Yeah, the instant will put hair on your chest. Do you have a signal here? I won't until I get closer to the house." Hell, she wasn't one hundred percent sure she had her phone with her. It could be at the farm. Who knew? She just needed to get her happy ass to the tree farm and make all merry and shit. She loved this. It was her bread and butter. "I open at ten, and it'll be slow with the snow, so I can do my dead-level best to help."

"No signal. Can you just...drop me in town? I can get AAA from there. And maybe a latte. This is...whoa. Thank you though." Charlotte set the coffee down. Her smile was less flirty this morning, more sweet. And tired.

"Of course. I'll take you to the house, get the dogs fed, and then we'll get you down the mountain." And if she couldn't do it, she'd send one of the teenagers with gas money and cash for doughnuts.

The kids were always willing to go buy food.

"You don't mind? I really appreciate it. I think the car is probably pretty stuck." Charlotte laughed, shaking her head. "And pretty dead."

"I don't. It's about a half hour to the house from here, give or take, and then half an hour down to the Springs." And it was seven? Six thirty? She just knew her babies were going to need feeding.

Charlotte crossed the room and found her boots. "You probably want to get moving. Are you going to have to run again? Can we both fit on the sled?"

"It's a one-person sled, but it's clear. Let me find you an extra pair of mitts too." God, this was weird and awkward, but that was what happened, she guessed, when you got yourself get all hot and sexy with a stranger.

"Oh. Thank you."

Charlotte took the mittens, and Lars suited up, taking the dogs outside to hook them up while Charlotte broke up the last of the fire so it would burn out quickly. It got a lot less awkward once they took off, Charlotte laughing and thoroughly enjoying the ride.

It was an easy, if bitter, drive home, and they pulled into the howling and hysteria of her secondary pack, who were losing their goddamn minds. She pulled in front of the A-frame that her granddaddy had built years ago to replace the old cabin. This house was decorated to the teeth, the Beckett Christmas Tree Farm sign filled with icicles. "Come on, I'll let you in the house, and you can check up with folks and warm up. I have to feed the puppers and make sure everything is ready for today."

"Oh I—uh. Okay. Sure. Thanks." It sounded like Charlotte was starting to feel the weird too.

"I'm not deserting you, promise. This is the busy season, hmm? And my guys need breakfast." She unhooked the dogs before she let Charlotte in the office-slash-meeting area. "There's a coffee maker with the good stuff and a powder room right there through that door."

"No worries. Thank you. Sorry to be...to impose." Charlotte went right for the bathroom.

"You're fine, pretty girl." Fine and wigged out. Lars needed to just get one of the teenagers to take her down to town. Either Brantley or Vicki would be in first. Draven— who thought of naming their son Draven? —was perpetually late, although that boy worked like a dog once he got in, so she kept him.

"Oh my god, Lars! Where have you been? Are you okay?" Vicky came jogging over to her, looking worried. "I fed this bunch, but they're all wigged that half the pack is missing. Were you out all night? That storm was crazy."

"I was. I stayed in Pappy's cabin. Picked up a lady that was stranded on the side of the road too." She beamed at Vicky. "Thank you for feeding the hooligans. I'm going to put them in the other pen and feed them right quick."

Ally and her team were howling and dancing and throwing a fit, and Lars knew her head was fixin' to explode. Just boom, and dogs would slurp up her brains.

"Ally, easy girl. Geez." Vicky jumped right in to help. "You look like you need coffee and a nap, boss."

"You know it, and someone's got to get the lady down the mountain so she can call AAA."

"Oh. I'll have Brant take her...want me to? He has that big truck." Vicky was good with the dogs. It wasn't technically her job, but she liked them, and she learned because she wanted to.

"Yeah, that'll work. That way we can get set up for the 'ooh, white Christmas trees, yay snow!' crowd." She winked, because she wasn't so much of a Scrooge, really, but she was tired and it was going to be a busy damn day. She still hadn't found the Christmas tree for the bazaar, for chrissake, and that was coming up.

"Right? They're pretty but my mom is like, hell no, we're not bringing a snowy tree inside." Vicky's dad had come and got their tree a week ago—dug it up with his back-hoe, roots and all. They brought it in for Christmas and would plant it somewhere on their land after the winter. Lars figured Vicky's family had to have a small tree grove of their own by now.

She nodded, but she also got it. Some folks were in love with the romance part of their holiday, and that was cool. Not only that, but today's sales should put the farm in the black, and the rest of the season was pure profit.

They got the dogs all fed and squared away, and Vicky ran off to find Brantley and his truck. Part of her would have liked to drive her damsel in distress into town herself, but there was work to be done and she was already behind.

Still, she needed to let said damsel know. She went in, stomping snow off her boots before heading for the coffee pot. "Hey."

"Hey. So I'm all set. AAA is going to meet me in town at Caffeine Ivy's and take me back up the mountain for the car." Charlotte looked relieved. She seemed like a woman who needed a plan.

"Excellent. One of my guys is going to run you down, if

you don't mind. I have to get ready for an insane day. Vicky's already fielded a dozen calls making sure we're open, and I have to get prepared." Which reminded her, she needed to have Brant get doughnuts.

"Great. Perfect. I'll get right out of your hair." Charlotte handed her back the mittens she'd borrowed. "Thank you for...everything." Oh, that was a pretty blush, turning the woman's cheeks a warm pink. Charlotte really did mean *everything*.

"It was amazing to meet you. Seriously. I hope you get where you're going." She went over to the desk and handed Charlotte a business card. Just in case.

Charlotte read it over and smiled, then put it in her pocket without offering a number in return. "You might have saved my life, Lars. It was more than good to meet you," she said just as Brant burst into the room, parka all snowy and cheeks pink from the cold.

"Someone needed a ride, boss?"

"Oh, that's me."

"Okay. Truck's warm." Brant held the door, letting in a cold breeze.

"Thanks again and good luck with your crazy day." Charlotte gave her a wave and left with Brantley.

Okay then.

Wild one-night snowy rescue sweaty sex achievement, unlocked.

Go team Lars!

"Okay, Vicky, you get the crockpot filled with cocoa, text Brantley with our doughnut order, and let's put the cookies out." They had shit to do, halls to deck.

"Boston cream and strawberry jelly..." Vicky started texting. "On to the cocoa. I put out the hacksaws and turned on the Christmas lights around the field. Think that will thaw them out?"

"I'll put out the portable heaters if there's a crowd. No reason to until then." Lars grinned at Vicky and handed her a belled Santa hat as the first customers of the day pulled in. "Ho, ho, ho, girl."

"Who you calling a ho, boss?"

She snorted. Some shit never changed.

5

It was almost noon when the tow truck driver dropped Charlotte and her suitcases off at the farm and, in that time, she'd learned three things. First, beige cars were hard to find in the snow. Second, red wine did actually freeze if it was cold enough. And third, not even the hottest random sex with a stranger could completely negate the stress of coming home for the holidays.

The truck pulled away, leaving her in the driveway with her bags and she looked around as the dust—or snow, in this case—settled around her, somehow knowing this was going to be the last quiet moment she had until the new year.

"Lottie!" Jacob came out of the house, arm casted at the elbow, and immediately took a tumble.

"Oh Jesus. Jacob?" She dropped everything and ran to him. God, she was so glad to see her brother, but all she could think was that this moment was an omen of the weeks to come. "Are you okay?"

"Yeah. I just—It's so good to see you." He reached for her, and she hauled his ass up. The one-armed hug was just as enthusiastic and goofy as always. "I just—Thank you. You're a lifesaver. I was just telling Oksana about you, and—"

"Who's Oksana?" Her mind swirled with a dozen answers—his astrologist, tarot reader, spiritual advisor, angel medium…

"She's my girlfriend!"

Oh, shit.

She did not roll her eyes, though it took everything she had not to. She tried to keep her tone neutral too. "You have a girlfriend?"

"I met her on Twitch. She's amazing. You should see her cosplay Clown Girl. We totally vibe."

Was any of that English?

She gaped at him and shook her head, trying to find some response to…all of that. Finally, she just gave up. "How is your arm?" She made her way back down the front steps to get her bags.

"Cold makes it hurt, but I did it up good. Mom says Dad's doing pretty well. How dead's the car?"

"Dead-dead, but I don't care. It was a rental, the only thing they had left on the lot on short notice." That was in her price range. And she was going to leave out the part about not getting four-wheel drive. "I can use Dad's truck." She was already getting a headache. She hauled her suitcases up the steps and into the house while poor brother held the door. Poor guy. He liked to keep busy—or he used to—and this had to be making him crazy. Then again, maybe he spent all his time on…what did he say? Twat?

That wasn't what he'd said, but the thought gave her a giggle and made her headache feel better.

"Is my room still my room?"

"Your room will always be your room, Lottie. Mom wouldn't have it any other way."

Okay, that made her feel better. She was on the second floor, in the room with the turret. There was a window seat, and a ladder up to the tiny garret that attached to the attic. She had used that room as a dollhouse, as an art studio, as a library.

She'd been happy here. Useless, but happy.

"I'm going to take my things up and...and then I guess we should talk about...stuff." The bazaar. The big event on their property every year that drew most of the town and brought in enough money to pay the mortgage. Mom wasn't here. Dad wasn't here. Jacob was one-armed and...tripping over his own feet.

"Yeah. Aunt Deenie has called six times already." They shared a fond but exasperated glance.

Aunt Deenie was sweet as sugar, and everyone loved her, but...she was a total trainwreck.

"No. No Aunt Deenie. Can you make coffee?" She dumped her coat and boots in the hall, then hauled her things up the stairs to her room. She walked in and looked around shaking her head. The place was like a time capsule. Mom had cleaned up, but everything else was pretty much exactly the way she'd left it.

She didn't have time for a walk down memory lane right now. That poster of the Cranberries would forever be cool, though.

She took a quick shower and put on clean clothes before heading back downstairs. She really didn't need Jacob asking why she smelled like dogs. Or sex. That lovely night felt like days ago already.

The house smelled like coffee and...muffins? "Did you cook?"

Jacob looked at her like she was insane. "Are you stupid? I bought them from the coffee shop yesterday. She takes orders from that Cheyenne's Creations thing, and I knew you liked the blueberry muffins."

Okay, that was actually sweet. "Aww. Thank you, stinky." She kissed his cheek and accepted the cup of coffee, doctored just how she liked it with lots of cream and sugar, and sat down at the table with a muffin. "Sorry, I really needed a shower."

"That's cool. I—I'm glad you're here. Dad's coming home in a few days, but he'll need tons of help. Mom's stressing the money. Aunt Deenie's hysterical. Then there's One-Arm Wonder Boy."

"Mom always stresses money, and Aunt Deenie being hysterical is just Tuesday." And Dad would be fine. Dad had to be fine. Period. "I'm sorry about your arm. Does it hurt?"

"Nah, not really. When it happened, I wanted to die. Also, there's a huge hole in the hay loft floor in the barn now."

"You went through the floor? Oh my god." She sipped her coffee, just glad he wasn't also in the hospital. She didn't think she could do this all alone and deal with that too. She reached out suddenly and took Jacob's hand. "It's good to be here with you. I miss you." It was good. She felt like she could breathe better around Jacob.

"I miss you too. Are you happy there? I mean, I know Denver is cool, but..."

She sighed as she looked into her coffee, then raised her left hand and waggled her fingers, showing Jacob her missing engagement ring. "I used to like it better."

"Yeah... Mom told me. Fuck her. I hope she gets boils on her ass."

"Yes. Thank you." Damn right. You go, brother. That was

what she needed, people reminding her she was better off. At this point she wasn't sure if she missed Rosalie at all. The ring had been pretty, though. "Fuck her. But Denver is a great place. You know, great apartment, great job...it's *great*."

Great. Jesus. Hopefully Jacob was on some good meds or something for his arm so he didn't see right through that.

One eyebrow lifted. Dammit. "Great. My arm's great. Dad's great. The bazaar's going to be great."

"Yes!" She jumped on that, because she needed the change of subject. "The bazaar is going to be amazing. Because I'm here. Right? So tell me what you guys have done so far. Do you have the checklist? Is it still running the weekend before Christmas?"

"It's the Friday, Saturday, and Sunday before Christmas. Then Mom agreed to have a big sing-along on Christmas Eve."

Of course she did. Well, a sing-along was easy enough. Maybe a bonfire. Marshmallows. Okay that was a no-brainer. The bazaar though... "Where's Mom's book?" Mom kept a planning book every year. It was usually a disaster, but it had names and numbers and dollar signs and it was a start at least.

"Right here." He pushed it over, and the sight of Mom's curly handwriting on the front of the notebook, complete with Christmas stickers, made her smile.

"Okay. Cool." She opened the book and skimmed through the pages. Tents, vendors, food, entertainment... everything had a section, but after that it was chaos. Probably chaos that Mom understood but it was going to take her a minute. And more coffee. "They'll be home in a few days you said?"

"Yeah. The big thing is all the phone calls from everyone. We have the dance school, the high school choir, the middle school and high school bands. Lars has to bring the tree and set it up. Someone has to deck it. Then there's the vendors."

"Wait." She blinked at her brother. "Lars?"

"Yeah. Lars Beckett owns the Christmas tree farm up on the mountain, sells the Christmas trees in the M&M Outfitters parking lot, and she provides the big tree for the bazaar. She's named after her grandfather."

Damn it. She didn't even need to ask if this Lars owned a dogsled. How many women owned a tree farm and were named Lars? And now Lars had a last name too.

"Is there more coffee?" She got up and went for a cup, even though hers was only half empty, just to get a few more inches between her and her brother before the twin-Spidey-sense kicked in about this too. Of course the hot dogsledder had a major role in the fucking bazaar...because why should she be allowed an uncomplicated fantasy one-night stand? Everything in her life had goddamn strings.

So what if she broke out in goosebumps when Jacob mentioned Lars's name? That didn't mean she wanted strings. That just meant...it just meant she was still tingly about the way Lars had tortured her poor nipples. Which, while she was thinking about it, were aching this morning in all the right ways.

Damn it.

She was not into tattooed women usually. And she didn't get off on butch athletes with callused fingertips especially ones that had those fingers on her buttons when they barely knew her. That was just...

Hot.

No. Nope.

Wait. Jacob was talking. "What?"

"I said can you bring me another muffin. Are you okay?"

"Yes. I just didn't sleep well, and I'm...hungry." She brought back two muffins.

"Didn't you want coffee?"

"What?" She looked into her cup. Damn. "Oh. Right. See? So tired." She stepped back to the coffee maker and filled her cup up, then sat again. "Okay. So. You'll deal with the whole tree thing, will you? It's...something you can handle. With your arm I mean. It's phone calls and...right?"

Jesus. *Get it together, Char.*

"Sure. Sure, no problem. She's not a bitch. A little bit of a wild mountain woman, but she's funny as hell."

"Yeah? Do you know her that well?" That would be all she needed. She sipped her coffee and turned pages in her mother's book, trying to keep it casual.

"I mean, she took over when her dad died." Jacob shrugged and grinned. "We've had a few beers. She's run a bunch of dogsled races."

"Cool. Cool." That dogsled ride had been so amazing. Freezing, yes. Almost painfully cold, but unlike anything she'd ever done. It wasn't playing anything safe. It wasn't following a plan. It wasn't anything but spontaneous and wild.

So...not her. And she'd loved that.

God, she needed to change the subject.

"So all these phone calls...does Mom call them back? Drop in to see them? Call a meeting? Do you know?"

"Mostly she calls. She goes to stores for prizes and to get vendors sometimes. I'm in charge of the heavy lifting, you know? Lift that barge, tote that bale." Jacob was no help. None. Zero.

"The heavy lifting? So I need to replace you too?" She sighed. "Okay. We can do this. We have to do this, right? The farm..."

"We have to. It's...well, you know. This place is important." Jacob looked guilty, honestly. "And I never really knew how hard it was."

She knew, but when she left everyone had something to do but her. Poor Jacob. He was a dork, but his heart was always in the right place. She took his hand. "They did it for years. We can do it now."

"I tried, Lottie. I swear. I am trying to make it okay." For a second, she saw pure fear in Jacob's eyes.

Oh shit. Okay. She was older by nine minutes, right? Big girl panties. "Hey. You can't do this by yourself. You did the right thing. You called me, and we're going to be a great team. Mom and Dad are going to be proud." She had this. She wasn't going to let Jacob worry, or Mom. She'd get the job done.

Somehow.

"Right. You and me, Wonder Twins. We can handle anything." Jacob took a sip of his coffee, and the liquid sloshed out on his fingers, just a bit. "Thank you for answering the phone."

She always answered the phone for him. He was the only person she'd never ghosted. "Are you okay, Stinky?" She slid over to a closer chair and handed him a napkin.

He took it, trying to clean off his hand using the table, so she helped. He was a good guy. He *was*. "I—I feel like a loser. You're all together. You have this great job in the city, and I can't walk across the hay loft without killing myself."

She rolled her eyes. "I am so not together. I'm just really good at pretending I am. So good I even fooled you." Jacob wouldn't say that if he'd seen her pounding on her steering wheel while drinking wine straight from the bottle last night. "You're not a loser. You only need learn to tell the Universe to fuck off sometimes."

He winked at her, and she got a smile. "Yeah. Yeah, that's easier with you here, Lottie."

"Right? Fuck off, Universe!" She grinned at him. She could stand to take a little of her own advice.

"Fuck off, Universe!" he repeated, and they both laughed, and the air in the kitchen got a lot lighter.

"There. So I think—" The phone rang and she chuckled as she got up to answer it. "And so it begins. Hello?"

"Good morning. This is Vicky at Beckett's Christmas tree farm, and I was—"

"Oh, hold on. I've got your guy." Really? She was being haunted by Lars. That's what she got for telling the Universe to fuck off. She handed the phone to Jacob. "Tree people."

"Vicky?" he mouthed, then he lit up like that proverbial tree. "Hey! Vicky! How's it going?"

She watched Jacob talk wondering how this was so hard for a guy that was friends with literally everyone he'd ever met. Then she pulled out her cell phone, opened her mom's book and plopped her finger down on a name. Ken Piles from the hardware store. Dad's best fishing buddy, who was also a banjo player. Did banjos do Christmas carols?

This should be good. She picked up her cell phone and dialed his number.

Time to get this show on the road.

Somehow.

6

Lars headed down to town, trailer in tow, Goober the sled basset next to her. She needed to resupply the downtown lot, get a caramel hazelnut latte and a chocolate croissant, and possibly buy a good book.

Goober looked at her and howled. Damn dog. Always knew what she was thinking.

"Right. A book and bones." She made the turn into town, popping her neck. "I hope the girls appreciate you, thinking about them."

She toddled along, parking beside of the grocery store where one of her sales lots was set up. "Time to make the doughnuts, huh, Goob?"

Her pappy had said that every damn time he went to unload the trees. Every time.

Goober waited patiently for his lift out of the truck, then followed behind her, supervising as always. Sasha and Mike came jogging over to help.

"Hey, Lars! Glad you're here. We're out of the eight footers." Mike flexed like this was all his doing.

Sasha rolled her eyes. "I just sold the last one."

"To Tucker Reide and his boys."

"Lars, you gotta see them. They were shorter than me in school last year, I swear."

"They're like a foot taller than you are now." Mike laughed, giving Sasha a playful punch in the arm.

"Shut up."

"I guess everyone is a foot taller than you though, huh?" Mike hadn't stopped giggling and Sasha, all five feet of her, dove for him.

"Oh, shit."

"Get 'em, Goob." She walked around the trailer, chuckling as basset hound howls filled the air, then a snowball whizzed past her with Goober in pursuit.

"We pulling all of these? Or are some going up to M&M?" Mike helped her drop the gate and started loosening the tie-downs.

"I'm hauling four to M&M, and then I'm going to drop a bunch of these wreaths for the downtown stores." She still had to coordinate with the bazaar folks too. "Y'all doing all right? Things going good?"

"Things are great. We're busy, and it's not killer cold out here today. Sasha's mom brought cocoa and cookies. Did you pick out the big tree yet?"

"I have it marked. I'm going to wait for a couple of days before the event before I cut it." She wanted it to stay pretty through Epiphany, if she could.

"Is it as big as last year?" Sasha threw her arms open wide.

"A touch narrower, a touch taller. I have a picture on my phone." She found the picture with the big red bow around the trunk of the chosen tree. The damn thing was gigantic.

"Ooh!" The kids admired it.

"Now it's really Christmas!" Mike shouldered a tree and headed for the lot with Goober howling at his heels.

"Don't trip over the dog, kiddo." She helped unload, made sure they had change and charged phones. "Okay. I'm going to walk into town and grab a coffee. Come on, Goob! Let's go."

"Later!" Mike and Sasha waved and got right back to work. Sure, she hired a lot of teenagers, but she paid them better than most for being outdoors, and they were loyal and worked hard. If they didn't, they weren't around long.

Goober the sled basset loped along beside her cart filled with wreaths, nose going a mile a minute.

"I bet there's a puppy cookie for you at the coffee shop, Mr. Goob." A puppy cookie for him, a decadent coffee for her. She waved to everyone she passed, handing out wreaths to folks who needed one.

Downtown wasn't big, but it was crowded, everyone finally getting out to run errands after that big snow the other night. Caffeine Ivy's was crowded; it looked like the line went right to the door.

"Damn, busy, busy." She peeked over to the pet-tio, catching sight of Kylie, one of the managers at the M&M. "Yo, Ky! Watch Goob for me while I'm in line?"

Kylie rolled her eyes and grinned. "Have I ever said no to Mister Ears and his paws of doom?"

"Not yet. Thanks. I'll grab my coffee and I'll be right back." There were heaters and blankets out there for the pups, and Kylie and her pup Sadie would spoil Goober to death.

She opened the door and went about two feet to the end of the line. The woman in front of her was tall and wearing a fancy coat—a long wool deal—and the woman in front of coat-lady was on the phone. "I haven't done the map of where each booth will be just yet; that comes last once we see where... Yes I can take a request but I just can't promise...sure. Why don't you email me, remind me that we spoke, and I'll send you a contract this afternoon when I'm in the office. Great. Thank you."

"She wasn't taking no for an answer." Coat-lady chuckled at the woman in front.

"No. I'm so sorry, it's so rude to be on the phone in line. Sorry. I just... I'm a little... I don't even have a real office." The voice seemed familiar, but the woman who turned around was unmistakable. "Do you know what a spitzbuben is? It sounds dirty right?" Charlotte's laugh floated on the air, just above the scent of roasted coffee beans.

"Thumbprint cookies," Lars answered, and damn if her voice didn't go all rough. So Miss Charlotte was staying in town? Good to know.

Not that it mattered. Charlotte had her business card. If she'd wanted to call, she would have.

"Thumb—" Charlotte's eyes went wide, and she laughed nervously. "Oh. Cookies. I should have known. Thank you." Charlotte turned her back as the line moved up, and for a second she thought that was it. Total cold shoulder. But then Charlotte shifted and let coat-lady go ahead of her. "Hello."

"Hey, there. How's it going?" Shit, she wasn't so good at the whole rules of engagement thing. She was way more cavewoman, grr.

"Good. Fine. Are you here for coffee?" Charlotte blushed suddenly, looking embarrassed. "Of course you're here for coffee. That was a dumb...uh." That sentence ended in a little chuckle and a shrug.

"Coffee, croissant, and a biscuit for Goober. I promised him." And that dog remembered.

"Who's Goober? One of your dogs?" The line moved up and they were so close. Almost there.

"Yes, ma'am. He's my basset. He lives in the house, so you didn't meet him." Although he loved to ride on the sled, his ears just flopping.

"Oh cool. My brother has bassets! Two of them—Ginger and Bailey." Charlotte blinked and Lars had to laugh, that bit of personal information had slipped right past the woman's pre-coffee filter.

She knew Ginger and Bailey; they were the Miller's dogs. Which meant Charlotte's brother was Jacob Miller. "Bassets are special beasts. Goob is their litter mate. Bonnie is an amazing breeder."

"Wow. Well…wow. So…small world. Okay then. My turn to order." Charlotte ordered herself a great big caramel macchiato.

Small world. Right. Apparently it hadn't been as… amazing as she'd thought.

"Lars. Let me buy your coffee?" Charlotte waved her up to the counter.

"Oh. Oh, you want to? I have to get a puppy biscuit." She grinned. "Maybe I should get yours."

"Nope. Any dog of my Dame with shining dogsled is a dog of mine. Or, well, you have a lot of dogs so I may qualify that in the future, but today you're good." And there was that smile again, the one that Charlotte had given her in the cabin that had warmed her in a way the wood stove couldn't.

She cracked up. "Well, then, I promised myself a caramel hazelnut latte. And thank you. Very much."

They took their coffees and breakfast to a table outside right near the heater. Goober padded right over and sat on Charlotte's boot. "So Jacob says your farm donates the big tree?"

"We do. I have one picked out. Do you want to see it?" They had donated the tree for this thing for as long as she could remember.

"Oh. I do, but... I have some errands in town and then I have all these phone calls to make and..." Charlotte sighed. "The bazaar..."

"Hey, pretty lady—" She went for gentle and easy, because Charlotte had to be stressed as hell. "I have a picture on my phone. How's your dad doing?"

"Oh, fine. He's fine. He'll be home in a couple of days." Charlotte stuffed a bite of muffin in her mouth and nodded.

"Good to hear." Lord have mercy. Charlotte didn't need a coffee. She needed a massage.

Charlotte smiled as she finished chewing. "I think Goober wants his cookie. He's putting my foot to sleep."

"Oh, sorry. Goob. C'mere, buddy. You want a bite?"

Those ears perked up, and Goob stood and wagged over. Food motivation, thy name was Basset.

"There's my good boy."

"He's cute. So I guess your family has been working with mine on this bazaar for a long time? I don't usually... Mom needs help this year."

"Since I was a little girl, for sure. Do you remember my pappy? Huge guy, white beard, played Santa for decades?" No one forgot her grandfather or his huge laugh, his bright blue eyes.

"I think so. To me, he was just Santa. I remember his beard was real, and he had those twinkly blue eyes. He was the real deal. Did your dad take over after that?"

"My dad was killed in an accident when I was twelve. He was cutting lumber with some other guys and a tree hit him." It had been long enough that saying it wasn't brutal.

Charlotte reached out and rested light fingers on her wrist. "I'm so sorry. I didn't mean to—that was—sorry."

That touch electrified her, buzzing through her. "It was very long ago but thank you. He was a neat man. He wanted to be my grandfather."

"You're named after him, right? Your grandfather? I mean, Lars is a big name."

"I was little Lars the whole time growing up, so it stuck. No one would know who you were talking about if you said Naomi Bennett." She winked over, like she was letting Charlotte in on a secret.

"Naomi." Charlotte grinned at her. "I like it." Those fingers moved away as Charlotte picked up her coffee again. "It's a good thing you found me before I became a popsicle up there. Jacob was in way over his head on this bazaar."

"Yeah? I heard he broke his hand or something? That sucks."

"His arm. He fell from the loft in one of the barns. Goofball. And Mom is with Dad and..." Charlotte caught her eye, not hiding the panic very well. "I've never done this before."

"Well, I have. At least sort of. And I am familiar with town." She didn't have a lot of time, but she had a little, and she had advice out the wazoo.

Charlotte squinted at her and leaned over the table. "Do you know Marge Kelly at the jewelry store? Is it me or is she...like, hard to talk to?"

"She's...an island. An island decorated in diamonds." That woman had issues that went straight to the bone, which started with her husband of forty years leaving her for his nineteen-year-old personal assistant. That boy had been trouble in a pair of stretch jeans.

"She has a booth at the bazaar. Mom was trying to get

her to donate something for the charity auction but wasn't having any luck. Do I play it cool and cute? Sassy city girl? Desperate, overwhelmed nutjob would be easy…play what you know."

"Just be honest. Seriously. She can scent a setup like a shark smells blood in the water." Lars rolled her eyes and grinned. "I'd tell the truth—Dad is sick, brother's broken, Momma's going to lose her mind, and I'm here helping."

"Oh god. I can't do that. That's like, pity party table for one, please." Charlotte shook her head. "That's not a good look."

"Well, then—" Okay, what would guarantee a donation? "Maybe call a vendors' meeting and just have everyone sign up for a giveaway there?"

She wasn't a vendor. She was just the tree woman. Hear her roar.

"Oh." Charlotte blinked at her. "Hey, that's a good idea. That's a really good idea."

She told herself that the shocked look didn't mean Charlotte was surprised that she'd come up with a good idea.

She had one or two a decade. Just ask her, she'd tell you.

"Excellent. I'm happy to help out."

"Thank you so much. Wow. You're brilliant." Charlotte's phone started to ring, and she pulled it out. "Sorry I need to…hello? Okay. Yes, I can… I'll drop by. Pick it up where? Beckett's Tree Farm? Got it." Charlotte smiled at her. "Yes, I think I can find it, dork. Love you, bye."

Charlotte put her phone away. "Jacob just added a couple more errands to my plate, one of which is stopping by this tree farm you might know to pick up three wreaths he ordered?"

"Ah. Well, I happen to have a wagon full of wreaths here, if it'll save your car..." She remembered that poor vehicle.

"Oh, god. That thing got towed away. I'm driving my dad's truck, And I'm guessing you don't have our barn wreath in your wagon? It's huge." Charlotte frowned. "Dad and Jacob usually put it up together. I'm like, half Dad's height."

"I do not. It's up at the farm." And Charlotte was right. There was no way she could get that wreath up, but Lars could. "I'll bring it down and help you get it hung, if you want."

"What? Oh... I don't want to...except..." Charlotte sighed. "Are you sure you don't mind? I'd owe you one. Thank you."

"Sure. Sure, you guys have had a run of bad luck, eh? Neighbors help out."

"Lars Beckett! Is that you? Have you given up abusing those poor animals?"

Oh, for fuck's sake. Seriously? Belinda the PETA Member came up with her vegan leather and her Meat is Murder sweatshirt.

"Yep. Haven't abused a dog in days."

The "bitch" was implied.

Charlotte looked down at Goober who was basking in a patch of sun and bent down to give him a scritch. "Man, he looks so abused. Are you abused, you handsome little man? Oh right there, huh? Better make up for all the neglect you're obviously experiencing."

Goober turned over, offering her his belly like the goofy slut-puppy he was.

"Yep. Brutally neglected. Viciously."

"You know very well I'm talking about those poor overworked sled dogs you keep up in your...your *compound*. Cruel is what you are."

"Cruel?"

"Cruel and abusive." Belinda crossed her arms. "She works those dogs like slaves."

"Whoa...whoa, lady." Charlotte pulled herself up to her full five-foot-nothing height and got right in Belinda's ugly face. Or close enough. "Look. I don't know who you are, but let me tell you something. Those dogs saved my life the other night. I was stuck in my car on the mountain road in the storm, and I didn't have any cell service. No rescue vehicle was going to find me. If it hadn't been for Lars and her brilliant guys, I'd be a popsicle up there instead of standing here talking to you. Those dogs are beautiful, strong, and very well-loved, I can promise you that."

Lars swore she saw little sparkles all around Charlotte, sparkles and little violets and the periodic bluebird. That was glorious.

"What she said."

"Well." Belinda tossed her head and tried not to look flustered.

"Uh-huh. Now move along, unless you'd also like to discuss my fondness for bacon."

"Rude." Belinda turned on her heel and marched back down the street where she'd come from.

"You are absolutely amazing." Lars was going to buy this beautiful girl a steak and watch her eat every bite.

Charlotte blushed. "Sorry. That was over the top, huh? You didn't need me to step in and rescue you, I know, but she just...ugh. Ugh! And with all this bazaar stress, I am completely out of patience and fake smiles."

"Want to come up to the house?" It was random, but she didn't require patience or fake smiles.

"I do have to get that wreath. But I have a few errands in town and all these phone calls, and..." Charlotte stuck out her lower lip and blew hair out of her face. "Oh, and Jacob is expecting me to talk with the tent people in a couple of hours. Can I come by later?"

"Of course. Do you need directions?" Because Charlotte hadn't exactly driven herself up or back.

"Uh...you want to text them to me? Give me your phone." Charlotte held her hand out like she was expecting yes for an answer.

She unlocked it and handed it over, the picture of the sled dogs and Goober right there for the world to admire.

She caught Charlotte smiling at the picture before entering info into the phone and handing it back. "There. Now you know how to reach me." Charlotte tossed her empty coffee cup and the garbage from their breakfast, then pulled on some gloves.

"Well, I'm going to deliver wreaths. Have a good morning. I'll text you directions to my place." And she'd buy something yummy to eat. Steak, maybe, or stuff for burgers.

"Sounds great." Charlotte tugged her stylish winter coat tighter and gave a little wave before marching off in her warm but still pretty boots.

Lord have mercy, that girl was a mixture of fierce and wide-eyed, and Lars was fascinated, stupid as it was.

"So, who was that?" Kylie winked over at her. "I thought I knew everyone in town."

"Charlotte Miller."

"Miller like the Cedar Ranch Millers?"

She snorted and nodded, but that was it, exactly. "Yep. I guess she's Jacob's sister."

"Huh. Good on you. She's cute. Have fun."

She tried for wide-eyed and innocent, but Kylie? She wasn't having it. "Okay, Goob. Time to hit the road."

7

C harlotte puffed out a breath and climbed out of her dad's truck. She wasn't getting any taller, and that wasn't going to get any easier. She went around to the passenger side and grabbed her bag, a bottle of wine, and a six-pack of beer before trudging up to Lars—Naomi's—front door.

She knew she shouldn't be here. She kind of wished she'd said no. It's not like she knew anything about anything right now—was she going to pull off this bazaar? Was she going to have a job when she went back to Denver? Was she even going back to Denver? This...whatever this was, was the last thing she should be getting involved with.

And what was this anyway? Somehow picking up a wreath had turned into a visit, and of course she couldn't come empty-handed so now it was a visit with alcohol.

She kicked the snow off her boots, climbed the front steps, then took another deep breath. Her hands were full, so she rang the doorbell with her elbow.

"Hey, lady!" Lars looked...sexy as hell in a pair of jeans and a green turtleneck that showed every inch of that taut body. And that was why she was here. She could lie to herself, but what was the point? Lars was stacked and gorgeous, and worse? She was smart and totally had her shit together.

Was there anything sexier than someone who had their shit together?

"Hey." She gave Lars a flirty smile at the same time she was mentally telling herself not to. "I didn't know if you were a wine or a beer girl." She held out both. "Choose your poison."

"I'm making steaks and baked potatoes. That's totally a beer meal." Lars winked at her and led her into the kitchen, which was homey and a weird mixture of simple and modern. The tiles were from the 70s, the floors were aged hardwood, the appliances were top-of-the-line and new.

"Mm. Meat! I can't wait to tell your friend in town." She winked at Lars as she put the wine and beer on the counter. "This is a great house. I love this kitchen."

"Thanks. I've put some work into it. I tend to have summer projects to keep me busy." Lars grinned at her, then winked. "My dogs aren't interested in moving in the summertime."

"Oh, man. No, I guess not. Do you shave them? How do they stay cool?" She wouldn't want to be a sled dog in July. Unless Lars was petting her. Then she'd be a happy puppy.

That was a sad analogy.

"They love to go to the river. Love it. And I have an industrial ice maker in the back." Lars's eyes actually twinkled. "They love rolling in kiddie pools filled with ice."

"Oh my god, that's so cute!" She shrugged out of her coat. "Should I hang this up?"

"I totally can. The coat closet is right here by the door, next to the powder room." Lars took her coat and hung it, and she caught a glimpse of markings with ages and dates next to them. Little Naomi, she wondered.

"Do you have any siblings?" She pointed to the markings. "Or are those all you?"

"All me. I was trouble enough, all on my own." The tone was light, but Charlotte thought she heard a little stress in there.

"You seem like you turned out all right to me." She watched Lars, loving how every move was so purposeful. Sure.

"I did. I'm living a decent life up here." Lars gave her a warm grin. "I've lived in this house my whole life, believe it or not."

She nodded. "I believe it. I was born here too, but you must be a little older than I am because I don't remember you from school." She didn't remember anyone from Lars's family either, which seemed so odd, though this farm was kind of way up here off the beaten path.

"I sort of left school early and got my GED. Then I got my Associates. Then I got my Bachelors." Lars laughed and headed back for the kitchen. "I love online classes, honey. They suit me."

"That sounds so much more chill than what I did. I mean, I loved college, but it's pressure too, you know? And I picked like, the most competitive field out there right now. Marketing? Ugh. So competitive." She had a feeling the pressure would be off before long. That happened when one got fired.

"Oh, wow. No. I am doing horticulture. I'm not a marketer. I grow things." Lars handed her a beer, took one for herself, and then leered, oh so dramatically. "I'd offer to show you my greenhouse, but that sounds like a come-on."

"Can I have both?"

Yep. That came out of her mouth.

And worse, she probably ought to be more embarrassed about that than she was. She was a fucking grown-up, damn it.

"Hell yeah. Can I start now?" Lars stepped right up into her space, cupped the back of her head, and leaned down. Charlotte could almost feel Lars's lips on hers. "Like right now?"

She flushed, head to toe, her whole body waking up, every nerve on fire. "Now's good. Please."

"Mmm...thank god." Lars pressed their lips together, capturing her moan in between them.

She flung an arm over Lars's shoulders for balance, trying not to come off as the trollop she kind of wanted to be right now. Lars had had a sip of beer and tasted like hops and honey, and she let Lars tease her lips open with a naughty tongue.

Of course, Lars found her ass with one hand, the touch warm, confident, drawing her in closer.

That whole dogsledder in the snow fantasy thing? This was just as good. She didn't need the fantasy, or anonymity, or any of it. Charlotte was just as dizzy now as she had been thawing out in Lars's arms the other night. She set her beer down, pleased that it landed on its end, and pushed her fingers into Lars's thick hair.

Lars kissed her like she meant it, like she was starving, and Charlotte was her own personal buffet.

She moaned, which anyone listening would reasonably interpret as *go ahead and tear my clothes off in your kitchen.* Her skin tingled everywhere Lars touched her, little shocks of electricity running through her, and she gave up trying to catch her breath.

Lars reached up, cupped one breast, thumb moving to nudge her—

BOOM.

Lars lifted her head, eyes wide.

BOOM.

Then the sound of barking literally filled the air.

"Motherfucker." Lars ran for the door, grabbing a pistol and a rifle on her way out.

"Lars?" She took a second to remember how to breathe, then ran out the door too. "Jesus, fuck it's cold." And had to look like she'd been in a fight with a wild animal. She got as far as the top porch step before she realized she didn't have boots on and leaned out as far as she could to see what was going on.

"Git! Git the hell out of here!"

Lars's eyes were the size of saucers, and she lifted the pistol, firing a flare up in the air, and suddenly Charlotte saw it.

A moose was between the house and the dog pens, and that thing was huge. Utterly gigantic.

She'd seen her dad tangle with a moose once or twice. Dad was a big guy, but they were dangerous when they got spooked, and he had a healthy respect for them. "Be careful!" she shouted. "I'll get my boots on." Like there was anything she was going to be able to do.

"Stay in the house. I can't let this bastard hurt my babies!" Lars glanced toward the pen, then toward the moose, who'd backed off with the flare gun. "Come on, man. I don't want to shoot you. I like moose."

Lars was talking to the moose.

Talking.

To a bull moose.

A conversation with a moose. Lars was so badass. It was

the hottest thing ever. She could just stay right here and let Lars doing her mountain woman thing keep her warm.

But.

"You want me to see if I can get the dogs inside?" Why was she offering to help? She was a chickenshit at heart. Lars was brave and totally had this by herself.

"No. They attack him, and he'll trample them. He's backing up. Just stay there, honey."

"He's enormous. Please be careful." She stayed where she was, watching the moose, listening to Lars talk the thing off her property.

By the time Lars came back to the house, she was pale and shaking. "I'm going to check the dogs. I'll be right back."

"Okay but wait." Charlotte threw her arms around Lars's neck. "Breathe for one second. That was scary."

"No shit. That was a fucking *moose*, honey."

"Are you okay? You're shaking. Get a coat before you go back out. Do you need help?" She let Lars go, but kept contact, one hand holding on to Lars's arm.

"You want to see the pen? They're well-behaved beasts."

So Lars was fine, it was fine, everything was fine, huh? Okay. She could play along. "I know they're well behaved, I slept three feet from them, remember? Let me get my boots on." She ducked back into the house and pulled on her boots, then grabbed her coat, and one for Lars.

Lars was out at the pen, shaking boards, checking everything. "—swear to god, I thought he'd got to you guys. You were so good. I was so damn scared he'd hurt you."

"Hey. I brought you a coat." He held it open for Lars. "I know, you're all tough and RAR! Who needs a coat? But humor me."

"I'm not feeling crazy tough right now." Lars turned to

face her, and there were tear tracks on her cheeks, and those hands were shaking. "So thank you for the coat."

"Hey, you did great." She helped Lars put it on. "You chased that big lug off, and your dogs seem okay. You were amazing."

"They are okay. I think he got lost and frightened. They can be brutal. They trampled a team of sled dogs at the Iditarod, you know?"

"They don't like feeling threatened for sure. Hey, you guys." Charlotte leaned over and gave one of the dogs a scritch and everyone got jealous, nosing in for their turn. "Oh, okay. I got you. And you...oh you're so pretty. Got you. Hey, puppy."

Fifteen dogs. Lars had fifteen dogs.

This was a thing?

She was laughing before she'd gotten to them all. "They definitely seem okay."

"They like you. Do you have any dogs of your own?" Lars squeezed her fingers. "Thank you."

"Me, no. I live in Denver. I'm never home, so it wouldn't be fair. I just come home every once in a while and play with my brother's pair." Every once in a very long while. Years this last time around.

"Do you like it? I've been a couple of times, but it's so... busy. I always feel like a rube."

"I like Denver. I liked going to college in Denver a lot. I'm not sure how much I like living in Denver now, but there's so much to do. And I work a lot, so sometimes I still feel like a tourist." She didn't mind that it was busy most of the time; it was more that it felt kind of impersonal. Not like here where she ran into someone she knew everywhere she went.

"Ah. That makes sense. You said you were in advertising?

That sounds exciting, creative." Lars didn't sound like she was being flip, even as she shored up a board in the dog pen.

"Marketing. A little different and...not. I do like it. I... might not have a job anymore, though. We'll see." She rolled her eyes. Why did she say that? This wasn't a poor Charlotte pity party kind of moment. "Did the moose kick that?"

"I think so, yeah. So you left here right after high school?" Lars glanced up at her, cheeks rosy. "Okay, that's fixed. Let's go in. I'm cold, and we have steaks to put on the stove."

"Yep. I spent the summer getting ready for college, and off I went. It's fucking freezing out here." She fell in next to Lars as they walked up to the house.

"I'll start a fire and warm us up. You've got a great story to tell now. You helped drive off a moose."

"Pfft. Not hardly. I stood here and watched you drive a moose off. By talking to it. Hey, Mr. Moose. Go home now." She bumped shoulders with Lars and dashed up the steps.

"That's me, the Moose Whisperer." Lars goosed her as they fought to get in the door, both of them cracking up.

"Ow!" She tugged her boots off again and hung up her coat. "What would you have done with a big ol' moose carcass if you'd had to shoot him?"

"I would have called Evie at the Lazy M. She has a truck, and she's a stud. Then she would have had her lady make, like, moose tartare or moose carpaccio or moose burgers." Lars winked at her, but the tone was a little more worried than not.

"I'm glad you didn't have to. He was pretty. And that rack was amazing. Terrifying, but beautiful." She took a breath. "We had beers right? Let me get them. Are we grilling or cooking the steaks indoors?"

"I've got a little grill pan I can heat on the stove. I've had enough outside time for right now." Lars winked at her, starting to defrost.

"Works for me." She headed back to the kitchen and snatched up their beers, bringing one back to Lars. She hadn't forgotten where they'd left off before *moose-us interruptus*, but she was relieved in a way that they'd moved into dinner mode. She didn't know what she wanted, and she didn't have time to look too closely right now.

Lars knelt down and started laying the fire, the motions sure and definite. This was a woman who had done this over and over, and it was surprisingly sexy, when she got right down to it.

"This is a neat house. That's a great fireplace. Is it a lot of work keeping the place up?"

"I guess? I mean, it's good work, and it means something, so yes, but I'm not hating it." Lars pinked and met her eyes. "That sounds stupid, doesn't it?"

She thought about that while she looked into Lars's pretty eyes. "No. It doesn't at all, actually. You sound like my brother. The farm is everything to him."

"Yeah, we've talked about that a couple of times. He's stressed about fucking it up."

She nodded. "He really is. So worried. I don't remember him having so much anxiety about it before." Probably because their parents had been healthy until this last year. Mom's weird bout with vertigo, and Dad's stroke...

"You start taking ownership, and it gets real, you know?" That sounded like the voice of experience.

"I guess so." Taking ownership wasn't Jacob's strong suit. To be fair, it wasn't really hers either; she just knew when shit had to get done. "I don't think we're ready for real yet."

"I hear that. I wanted to spend another five years racing with the dogs full-time. I was pissed."

"That sucks." When people met the way she and Lars had, and didn't expect more than one time, or one night, no one asked a lot of questions, so she felt like they were coming at things a little backward. "How long did you race? I didn't even know that was a thing around here growing up."

"Okay, so that's a silly story." Lars went to the kitchen as she talked, obviously comfortable in her space. "In high school I was into this girl from Alaska. Like deeply into her. She told me she liked femme girls, so I started wearing makeup and had an allergic reaction. She told me she liked vegetarians, so I stopped eating meat."

Lars lifted the steak up and wiggled it. "But bacon! Then she liked dogsledding, so I started working on building a team so that I felt closer to her. I thought it would make her like me more, because I was a teenager and dumb. So, first there were Stone and Thorn—my first two dogs, and I was in love—and not with AlaskaKitty102. When Pappy hooked me up with a used sled, and I went to some training in Steamboat? I was caught."

That was a great story. "I would never have given up bacon, not even for AlaskaKitty102. The things we do for love, right?" She laughed, remembering some of the things she'd done. "But imagine if you hadn't? This whole dogsledding thing was obviously because you were meant to rescue me on the road the other night."

Lars snorted softly, but the nod at Charlotte's words was immediate. "It was fate. I normally would have never driven that close to the road."

"I got the better end of the deal. I apologize. I'm a total

train wreck with a big mouth." She winked and sipped her beer.

"You were the most adorable thing I'd ever seen—all big eyes and curls."

She stared at Lars for a second, then turned her head and blushed, warmth creeping up from her chest to her cheeks. She couldn't help her embarrassed smile. "You were this strong, sexy stud, and you ran through all that snow in that awful weather...you were amazing. It was the hottest thing ever."

"No. The hottest thing ever happened in the hunting cabin." Lars sounded very sure about that.

That was the truth. They almost burned the cabin down despite the snowstorm. She glanced back at Lars, nodding slowly. "Yeah. Yeah, that was...wow."

"It was." Lars licked her lips, and that suggestion was simply...unavoidable. "How do you like your steak?"

"I—" She cleared her throat. "Rare, please." She ran her fingers up Lars's arm. "Like you."

"Oh, that was...that was nice. Can the cook have a kiss?"

"I don't know. If I kiss you, my steak might overcook." But who was she kidding? She cared more about the kiss than dinner. She stepped in close and went up on her toes, offering anything Lars was looking for.

Lars leaned down, kissing her hard enough that her ears rang a little bit, putting an hour's worth of making out in a connection that lasted a minute.

She held onto Lars even after it ended so she didn't fall over. "Whoa...dizzy." Now she understood what people meant when they said swoony.

"Mmm... I love the way you taste." Lars's voice went all husky.

She was caught in this strange space between panic and

lust—just completely frozen. Nobody had ever taken all her self-control with a kiss, not ever. She didn't even know that was a thing that could happen. "I have no idea what I'm doing." The words just popped out of her mouth. "I'm not even sure what that means. I'm... I don't even know."

"Well, let's have supper. I made potatoes, and there's salad and steak. That's a plan."

She nodded. "It's a good plan." Had she hurt Lars's feelings? Or was Lars being cool while she was being neurotic? She couldn't tell. "Thank you for inviting me. It's already been...wonderful. Even with the scary moose."

Wasn't she supposed to be picking up wreaths too? Maybe she'd do that tomorrow.

"Hey—That wasn't blowing you off. That was you seemed like you needed a second to breathe." Lars brushed a curl off her forehead. "I'm winging it too."

That gentle gesture had her smiling again. "Yeah? Really? Okay. You're right. I do need to breathe, or something. I just didn't expect...this. You. Meeting someone was the last thing I was thinking about when I came home." She touched Lars's elbow. "And that's not blowing you off either."

"Then we're okay. Steaks. Beer. A fire. Maybe...more?"

"I'm in." She nodded, and her stomach growled. "Apparently I'm hungry."

"Steaks are good for that, I hear. Let me flip them." Lars turned the steaks, and damn, they smelled delicious.

"So nobody calls you Naomi, huh? Nobody?" She liked the name a lot. "I mean, it's sexier than Lars..."

"Nobody. I was Little Lars for my whole life." Lars's cheeks went bright red.

There went her big mouth again. "Did I embarrass you? It's just that I like Naomi. It suits you."

"Embarrassed? No. No one's ever said that before. To me, I mean."

"That Naomi is sexy?" She leaned in and kissed Lars—Naomi's cheek. "It is. I like it. Can I use it?"

"I—Yeah. Yeah, you can." Naomi's cheeks were warm, and the kiss she got was bordering on hot.

She'd almost been married, so obviously she'd thought she understood what a real connection was, what real intimacy felt like. What romance felt like. Except she'd never experienced any of this. She'd never been so fascinated and so drawn to anyone. "Naomi," she said softly, fingers resting on Naomi's cheek. "Is it weird to hear it? Do you like it?"

"It's special. Like something that means something, you know?" Those eyes stared right into her.

"It means a lot; it's your name. It's yours. It's how I see *you*." Little Lars might have taken over the family business, but this woman was more than that one.

Naomi stole another kiss—this one hard and lingering, burning her lips and making her lips swollen—before rescuing the steaks.

"Damn, girl. Maybe we should have just scheduled a bootie call," she joked, breathless from Naomi's kisses. It was a joke, because while she probably would have accepted, this was much better. Overwhelming and dizzy-making, but better.

"That can be next. I want to make sure you're full of energy."

"Mhm. I'm going to need it to keep up with you. You keep trying to make me hyperventilate." She rested a hand on Naomi's ass, making it fit right into her palm.

It was hard, proof of hours and hours of work, and she

loved the way the muscles jerked and tightened under her fingers.

"So strong." She gave it a squeeze and took her hand away. "Should I take the potatoes out?"

"Please. There's hot pads hanging up next to the oven."

And sure enough, they were old and raggedy and well-loved. One or two might have been gnawed on. They could have been the ones hanging in her mother's kitchen. New could be good. Old memories were sometimes better.

She pulled out the potatoes and set them on a thick wooden cutting board, then hung the potholders back up. "Rar. Meat and potatoes." She took a goofy body-builder pose.

"There's a salad too. I have Italian and ranch dressing."

"Oh, ranch for me please." She went to the fridge to look. A little space between her and her hotness the grill master seemed like a wise idea. "In the door?"

"In the door. The salad's in that orange bowl."

The fridge was hilarious—the entire bottom shelf was labeled "dog food" and dated. Then the next one was leftovers. Then the top was chocolate milk, chocolate syrup, and a chocolate pie from the City Market.

"Someone likes chocolate." She took out the salad and the ranch dressing and set them on the counter. "I approve."

"Someone loves chocolate. I have a stash." Oh, that was a wicked smile, and Charlotte responded to it, wholeheartedly.

"Mmm. Good to know. Where are we eating?" She could take the salad and stuff to...wherever.

"Let's sit at the table. It's hard to cut steak on your lap, yeah?"

She nodded and took the salad out to the solid dining table, which had a nice view of the fireplace. She was just about to ask where the hound was when Goober sighed and groaned in his sleep, stretched out in a dog bed near the fire.

Oh, that was cute as hell—this floppy-eared beast enjoying his fire, relaxed and easy in his loose skin.

"Goober looks very happy about that fire," she said as she got back to the kitchen. "I didn't hear him barking at the moose. I wonder if he didn't know?"

Lars shook her head. "I'm not sure, but I'm grateful. Maybe he's developing a sense of his own mortality."

That made her chuckle. "My brother's dogs are lazy. It works in their favor sometimes. Can I carry something else?"

"Grab the steak knives? I'll bring the other silverware. Butter, sour cream, cheese on your potato?"

"Steak knives. This is a classy joint. I like it." She scooped them up. "And yes to everything on my potato." Everything. Bacon. Broccoli. Chives. Bring it on.

"Cool. I'll hook you up." Naomi pulled out tubs of butter and sour cream, cheese and bacon bits. It was casual and natural and totally appropriate.

"Do you cook a lot? I'm hopeless. I made spaghetti for Jacob last night, and I overcooked the noodles. That's just sad." She'd burned the garlic bread too, but she didn't need to get into that, right?

"I do. There's no delivery up here. I don't do anything fancy, but I do like to eat." Naomi sat and smiled over at her. "My favorite thing to make is beef stew. I love it."

"I love stew. And food. Eating is good." She was kind of a one-meal-a-day person, but that one meal was a no holds barred type of situation. Like this steak. Her mouth watered just looking at it and it smelled amazing. "I can't wait to dig into this."

"Go for it. I don't stand on ceremony." Naomi doctored her potato and offered her the salad with a smile.

"I will. It smells so good." She took a bite before dealing with the potato or the salad or anything because she just couldn't wait. Naomi had seasoned it so well; it was just a little peppery and cooked perfectly and the savory taste of the beef absolutely satisfied the carnivore in her. "Oh, Naomi. This is the way to my heart, let me tell you. Mmm." She took one more bite, reaching for all the potato fixings as she chewed happily.

"Ah, my dear carnivore." Naomi gave her a wink, and one stockinged foot slid along her calf.

"That's me." She smiled, but then worried about that *my*. Was that my like "mine"? And shouldn't that freak her out more? "That lady was so rude." She rolled her eyes. "Too bad she wasn't here to see you protect your pups from that moose. Ugh."

"Oh, she'd have tried to put a bow on one antler, and then bitched because he wasn't pleased."

"Some people." Her grin turned into a giggle and then into an outright laugh.

"Exactly. Like my baby dogs are abused! You saw the sheds. They live well. They're athletes." Naomi tossed her head, those brown eyes sparking with outrage.

"That's what I said, right? They're beautiful. God, you're hot when you're mad." She blinked. "Oh. I said that out loud, didn't I? I better put this steak knife down."

"You did. I am? I'll take it." Naomi caught her bottom lip in her teeth. "I thought you were the prettiest thing I'd ever seen, out there in the snow."

She gave Naomi a flirty grin. "Surely I cleaned up prettier."

"You're beautiful now, less wild. I'd love to see what you look like in my bed."

"Oh." She flushed, heat spreading into places you didn't talk about at the dinner table. Naomi's eyes never left her, and it wasn't uncomfortable at all. "Well...like me, only with a big ol' belly from this amazing dinner."

Naomi chuckled softly. "I think my view would be a little different."

Who would have thought that a Christmas tree farmer slash dogsledder would be such a flirt?

"I feel like maybe you're secretly a little bit of a player, Naomi," she teased. "You don't talk like a tough, secluded mountain woman."

"No?" Her eyes went wide, so comic, so adorable. "I am something of a hard-ass, but I do like a little bit of a tease."

She looked down and cut herself another bite of steak, then lifted it to her lips. "I like a little bit of a hard-ass."

"We might get lucky then. Again." Naomi took a bite of potato and hummed. "Yummy."

They ate and flirted, and every so often Goober would groan and stretch by the fire, and this was the most relaxed she'd been in months. Even the food tasted better than anything she'd had in all that time. She hadn't planned to stay the night, but she'd thrown a few things into a bag that was sitting in the truck just in case. Always be prepared, she'd told herself.

"Seriously, this was so good. I'm just—" The theme to *Iron Man* started playing and she sighed and dug in her pocket for her phone. "That's Jacob. What the hell could he...at this hour?" She looked at the phone and considered not answering it.

"Maybe he's protecting you from the Lesbian of the Mountain, dun dun dun!"

She was laughing as she answered. "Hey, bro, what's up?"

"I need help."

She glanced up at Naomi and she knew instantly that her overnight bag wasn't going to be leaving the truck. "What happened?"

"I'm...stuck in the bathroom."

Oh Jesus Christ. "You're what?"

"I can't get the bathroom door open, the handle came off in my hand and I only have one arm, you know? And I was about to take a shower so I'm naked too and—"

"Wow. TMI, bro."

"Oksana says you have to open the door from the outside."

She was tempted to suggest that Oksana do it, but she hadn't asked where Jacob's girlfriend lived yet, and she wasn't sure she wanted to know.

"I'm sorry, I know you're on a date and—"

"It's not a date." Was it? She looked at Naomi. "Is this a date? My brother has locked himself in the bathroom."

"It's a date. Are you serious? On purpose or by accident?"

"Accident. He broke the doorknob."

"I didn't break it," Jacob protested. "It just broke. I've been trying to fix it for an hour but it's a two-handed job I think, and I'm—"

"I know. Okay." Seriously? "He's only got one hand right now, and he's naked."

Jacob made a strangled sound. "Don't tell her that! Why did you tell her that?"

"She can't see you, idiot." How was this her life?

"I don't care, either. Penises aren't on my love map, man." Naomi wasn't helping.

"Ew." Jacob didn't have a penis. He was her brother.

"Lottie! I really need help."

"Okay, okay. It's not a short drive though, and it's dark so you better be patient."

"I have a magazine."

"No! Don't tell me that! Ew!" That she couldn't un-see. Un-hear. Whatever.

"Just make sure he's got toilet paper and air freshener."

"Naomi!"

"Who the fuck's Naomi?" Jacob sounded affronted. "I thought you were into Lars."

"I am. They're the same person. It's a long story. How is this your business? Where does Oksana live anyway?"

Dammit.

"Salt Lake. She's at BYU. Twitch remember? We cosplay?"

Naomi tilted her head. "Is that what straight boys call it these days?"

She covered her mouth to keep from barking out a laugh and shook her head at Naomi.

"Hello? You still there?"

"Sorry. Yes." She swallowed, still grinning, and pointed to Naomi, mouthing "Naughty."

"So are you coming?"

She sighed. "Not anymore."

"What?"

"Yes. Yes. I'll be home soon. Are you okay?"

"All I wanted was a shower." Jacob sounded so sad all of a sudden.

"I know. Just relax. I'm on my way."

"Thanks, Lottie. I appreciate y—"

She hung up, rolling her eyes. "So, this isn't how I'd hoped this would end."

"No, me either. Are you okay driving down to save the naked boy?" Naomi didn't seem mad, more…resigned.

"Yeah, I'm okay. I'm really sorry. I'd say come home with me but…dogs. Can we pick this up again soon? Like, right here?" Skip the meal and get right to how great she'd look in Naomi's bed.

"Absolutely. Just call. I will answer."

"I'm so sorry." She hopped up from her seat and sat in Naomi's lap. "I will call." She gave Naomi a kiss that made it clear she was for real. "I promise."

"And I believe you. My bed's waiting." Naomi cupped her breast, thumb sliding over her nipple.

She pulled herself away from Naomi, muttering about how life wasn't fair. Because it wasn't, dammit. But as she pulled away in the truck, she realized that she was supposed to be bringing wreaths home with her, so at least she had a reason to call Naomi very soon.

Tomorrow, maybe.

Maybe. After they got Mom and Dad settled. Fuck, that really was tomorrow.

She was never going to get everything done.

8

"Boss! We're out of twine!"

"Boss! We need cocoa!"

"Boss, they called from the downtown stall, and they're out of four or seven footers."

"Boss!"

Lars was going to change her name to "Not the Boss" or "I Fucking Hate Christmas Today" or "Please, I have the equivalent of blue balls".

Was that blue ovaries?

Okay, that was vaguely unnerving.

She needed to be three people today, and when Charlotte's text came in, she wished she could be four.

CHARLOTTE:

Hey, gorgeous. I really need those wreaths. Should Jacob and I come pick them up?

I have to bring a load of trees down in an hour. You can meet me then or you can come up this evening or I can come out and help hang them.

It really depended on how much help versus sex Charlotte needed.

CHARLOTTE:

Can you come help? My dad just got home and things are crazy.

Sure, honey. I'll be there @4ish.

Yeah. Dads weren't conducive to sexy times...

CHARLOTTE:

Thank you! The bizarre tent went up today, it looks great. Everything under it is going to be a disaster, but it'll look amazing.

Lars had a little giggle. The bizarre bazaar. She loved it.

It will be fine.

CHARLOTTE:

Clearly you haven't known me long enough. It will be good to see you at 4 tho.

U need anything from town?

Coffee? Cookies? Hot lumberjack in flannel?

CHARLOTTE:

Wine. Valium. Or if you can find one, a hot dogsledder with some time on her hands.

Wine. Dogsledder. Chocolate. On it.

She'd ask one of the kids to feed for her, and Goob could ride to town with her. They were basset friendly at the farm.

CHARLOTTE:

You're so sexy when you just handle shit.
See you soon.

Breathe, honey.

Lars chuckled and poured more cocoa into the Crockpot. First, load trees, then dogs, deliver trees, pick up goodies, charm the parents, seduce the girl.

No problem.

Maybe she should go change her underwear...

CHARLOTTE:

I'll try.

"Boss!" She rolled her eyes, but one of the teenagers held out her keys. "Trailer's all loaded up."

"Can someone feed the beasts for an extra twenty in their pay envelope?" Someone was always ready.

"I'll do it." She got two takers. "We'll split it. You want us to lock up after closing?"

"Yeah. I'll drop this off, and then I'm going to run to the farm to hang the wreaths for the bazaar." She winked over. "Jacob has a broken arm."

"Uh-huh. And the twin sister is *hawt*!"

Vicki rolled her eyes and slapped Draven on the back of the head. "Why is it always about booty for you?"

"Ow!" Draven cringed, grinning.

"Always!" Vicki almost managed to hide her grin. "Perv."

"Am not! I've got a healthy libido."

"Boss doesn't care about your libido! She just wants the dogs fed." Vicki winked at her.

"I do. I want the dogs fed and adored. *Adored*." She grabbed her scarf. "I'll provide breakfast in the morning."

"We got it, boss. They'll get all the love." Vicki bumped

shoulders with Draven who fell over in the snow dramatically. She knew her babies would be well loved on. Hopefully the rest of the place would still be standing in the morning.

Honestly, she had amazing employees, and most of them started in high school and came back for winter break all through college. It made for relationships and neat stories, and it gave her something to laugh about during the totally silent times she had from January to the spring thaw.

"Say hi to Jacob's sister for me!"

Vicki tackled Draven, and they ran off toward the dog pens.

She loaded Goober into her truck, and they headed downtown to restock the lot. They were having a great season, and some of the fancy-assed folks would come in for the bazaar and buy trees. She was feeling confident about being able to afford to take on a few races this winter.

She couldn't wait.

The lot was busy, and she got there just in time. Her crew started unloading and tagging trees as soon as she pulled up, and she headed up to check the till and see if they needed change. The light snow made the lot look festive, and people were milling around, enjoying their cider and snacks while they shopped.

"You heard that the Millers' daughter is actually running things this year, right?"

"Charlotte? I thought she was a marketing biggie in Denver."

Naomi wasn't an eavesdropper as a rule, small town gossip wasn't really her thing. But when Libby Turner mentioned Charlotte's name, that got her attention.

"That's the one."

"I guess she's got time on her hands now that she's not engaged anymore."

Oh, lord. She was going to have to find out about that. There wasn't any reason to feel lied to, because Charlotte hadn't, but Lars was crazy curious about all the parts of Charlotte's life.

"Oh, her poor family. You know they'd been planning a June wedding at the farm. It's all Victoria talked about last summer. She had it all planned. The dresses were going to be silver, and the flowers were all going to be blue."

Libby chuckled. "Well, no one's ever going to marry Jacob. He's...a free spirit. He'll be a glorious bachelor for years to come."

"Small wonder they broke up. The way her mother talked about it, that girl worked constantly. Hardly ever made it home. Swooping in now? It's got to be a boost for her career, or she wouldn't do it, right?"

Libby snorted as they moved away. "Wouldn't be a bit surprised."

Lord have mercy. She fought the urge to start singing "I Kissed a Girl" at the top of her lungs, just because she could, and it would be incredibly true.

Still, fiancée? Biggie wow city job she could leave for a few weeks? Fascinating.

The ladies were laughing now, and it was hard not to wonder what about, even as much as she wanted not to care. Thankfully, one of her teenagers tapped her on her angel shoulder, silencing the devil on the other one. "Are we tagging the wreaths too, boss?"

"No, those are for the bazaar. I'm running them over now." After she grabbed chocolate, wine, coffee, and possibly some sort of food thing for the family. Something heart healthy.

"You need any help?" Will popped up eagerly. "I know Jacob; he's a gamer."

"Nah. I got this. I'm going to do a few errands and take Goober over to visit while I hang them." And possibly share a few wine-soaked kisses, if she was lucky.

"Okay, boss. Thanks for the restock!" Will jogged back to the booth where a line was starting to form.

Sell sell sell, little trees. Buy more dog food and wine.

The trailer was lighter with only the wreaths in the back, but the snow was heavier as she made her way out to Cedar Ranch and to Charlotte. That didn't stop Ginger and Bailey from plowing through it to greet her truck as she pulled in.

"Hey, guys!" She let Goober out to play while she grabbed the goodies—three-foot-long sandwiches, a bottle of merlot, and a chocolate mousse cake. By the time she got to the door, Jacob met her, the cast on his arm huge. "Dude! Impressive."

"Right? Go big or go home." He grinned and gave her a quick hug with his good arm. "I'd offer to help carry but..."

"No worries. I brought something easy to eat for everyone."

"And chocolate and wine for Lottie. Good woman." Jacob winked at her, and she dipped her chin.

"I try."

"Come on in." Jacob opened the door for her and held it. "Thanks for helping Lottie deal with those wreaths. I'm just...useless."

"You are not useless. Will you stop saying that? Hey, you." Charlotte gave her a smile and helped gather things and take them to the kitchen. She looked frazzled—hair in a messy bun, sweatpants, no makeup. "Thanks for—"

"Charlotte!"

Charlotte tossed her head back and groaned, then lifted it again. "Coming, Mom!"

She got a kiss on the cheek, and Charlotte was off again.

"See? Useless. You want some coffee?" Jacob put the sandwiches in the fridge.

"Nah. I'll go hang wreaths. Point me toward the ladder?" She could make herself useful, because damn, she wasn't ornamental.

"Wait! I'm coming." Charlotte appeared in tall snow boots, tugging on a white down parka. She glanced at Lars as she fought with the zipper. "I'm here. I'm good."

"Mom's good?" Jacob sounded surprised.

"If she calls, tell her I'll be back in a little while."

"Okay."

Charlotte straightened up and plastered on a completely fake and frazzled smile. "I'm ready."

"Okay, honey. Let's do this thing." Someone needed some time away from her mom, that was for sure. "Where's the ladder?"

"In the barn. The big wreath goes up on that one so we can start there. The smaller ones are easy." Charlotte followed her out the door. "Oh, thank god. I needed out of the house. Between the bazaar and my dad, my mother is driving me insane."

She wouldn't be happy in that mess, that was for sure. "How's Deenie? She's your aunt, right? Surely she can help?"

Lars almost kept a straight face.

Charlotte raised one finely shaped eyebrow. "Deenie is smart enough to stay away." Charlotte held the look for a few seconds and then grinned and shook her head. "That's a whole other mess I don't need."

Lars chuckled. "Oh, honey. I know about Deenie. She's a sweetheart, but a bit of a flitterer."

"I adore her in small doses on unimportant occasions." Charlotte stuck a hand in her coat pocket. "I'm glad you're here. Thank you for coming to the rescue. Again."

"I will be your knight in blue metallic armor at least through Christmas. I guarantee it." After Christmas, she was just a dogsledding farmer.

Charlotte led her out to the big party barn, opened it with a key, and flipped on the lights. The outside lit up with a couple of warm flood lights, but the inside was lit with long strands of string lights in a crisscross pattern all the way to the other end, and a jumble of fairy lights around the door frame. "The big ladder is there. You see where the wreath needs to go?" Charlotte pointed to the open space above the door. There's a big, strong hook already there; it stays there year-round."

"Cool." She could handle that. She set the ladder up, shouldered the big wreath, and climbed up. "You tell me when it's straight."

She chuckled at her little private joke, and then loaded the wreath onto the hook.

"You mean the wreath, right?" Charlotte backed up to get a better look. "Because there's no hope for you."

"No? No chance that tomorrow I'll be into the almighty peen?" She laughed any harder, and she was going to fall off the ladder.

"Not as long as you're with me." Forget falling off, Charlotte's tone threatened to burn the ladder down.

"Then I'm safe as houses." Because Charlotte did it for her, to the bone. She tilted the wreath a little to the left. "How's this?"

"Um…" Charlotte moved her head one way and then the other, then backed up a few more steps. "A little more to the right? No, wait. That's left. Left. Sorry."

Left. She tilted it again, a little deeper this time, and one of the branches caught a little, making her rock on the ladder. Charlotte ran back and held her arms up like the poor woman might try to catch her if she fell.

"Easy! Easy. Are you okay? That's fine. It's good. Come down."

"I'm fine. The branch caught. It looks okay?" She slid down the ladder into Charlotte's arms. Oh, that did feel good. "I have four more to hang."

"Yes. But first I'm going to take a second to be relieved you're on the ground on your feet and not your ass. My whole family is medically challenged right now; if I'd had to add you to the list I would definitely think I was bad luck."

"You weren't here for any of it. Don't stress, honey. I'm good as gold." And her hands found that sweet ass, making her sigh as she squeezed. Yum.

"Doesn't matter. Somehow it's always my fault anyway." Charlotte gave her a wink and leaned into her hands. "The other four wreaths are easier. Two in here, one on the lamp post and one on the front door."

"Perfect. I should get a reward for hanging the big wreath." She drew Charlotte in tight. "Kiss me?"

"I don't know, should I? I mean, I did stop you from risking your neck any further, so maybe I should get the reward?" Charlotte licked her lips, gaze falling to hers.

"Mmm... I can do that." And she did. She started sweet and slow, but that didn't last long at all. Lars needed, and she felt like Charlotte did too, so she deepened the kiss, sparks lighting behind her eyes.

Charlotte melted against her, fingers curling into the lapel of her coat and holding on. Everything about Charlotte said green light—go.

Maybe they could lock the barn door and stay away

from the windows. No one would miss them for as long as it took for shared orgasms, right?

It was gratifying to find that Charlotte had the same idea. She dragged Lars into the barn and around the corner where they couldn't be seen. "The fairy lights make your eyes sparkle."

Her cheeks went hot as fire. Damn. "I want to take you home and unwrap you on my bed."

"Yes. Soon. Not tonight, but soon." Charlotte moved her scarf from her neck and hot lips found the exposed skin, speaking between kisses. "For now we have this super-sexy, freezing-cold barn. Next best thing, right?"

"Mmhmm. We seem to have freezing cold and super sexy as our thing, honey." She didn't fight her moans, letting Charlotte hear her pleasure, learn her hot spots.

"You warm me up." Charlotte's tongue tasted the soft dip at her throat. "Deep inside."

Lars didn't understand how Charlotte got to her so easily, so well, but it was a simple fact, and she wasn't going to argue with it. Each touch of Charlotte's tongue echoed in the pit of her belly.

Charlotte paused as they heard the sound of the big ladder being set down in the big room, and then the lights went out. "Oh. Shit." A second later the big sliding barn doors started to rumble closed.

"Hey, there! We're in here!" She called, trying not to groan. Her nipples were cut enough to poke through her bra.

"Hello?"

Charlotte sighed and rolled her eyes. "It's us, Jacob. Me and Naomi—uh, Lars," Charlotte called back, then whispered, "Fuck."

"Oh! Sorry, I thought I'd help, I figured you'd be out hanging the other wreaths."

"Sorry." Charlotte gave her a quick kiss, then stepped through the barely open barn doors. "Yep! Yep. That's what we're doing. Hanging up wreaths. The big one looks good, right?"

"Uh-huh. Dude, Lars. You're getting jiggy with my sister."

Wait. What? Lars stared at Jacob. "I'm doing what? What are you, a visitor from 1998? Are you going to show up with a Furby? An iMac?"

"Dude, Lottie had a Furby!"

Charlotte sighed. "I hated that thing. All it did was sneeze. It drove me crazy. Jacob and I used it for softball practice one day."

"She hit it way over the barn." Jacob nodded.

"Too bad there wasn't a scout there."

"Did the fur come off?" She fought the gales of laughter. She'd seen that on YouTube. The scary, furless Furby of Doom.

"I don't remember. I was laughing too hard. And then Jacob tried to—"

"I tried to go after it," Jacob interrupted. "And twisted my ankle—"

"And I ended half-carrying you back to the house."

"And Mom made popcorn."

"That was the first time we saw that movie—uh...the black and white uh—"

"*Psycho*!"

"Yes! And we watched *Psycho*." Jacob and Charlotte grinned at her, and even though they weren't identical, the resemblance was uncanny.

"Because that's not unnerving." But cool, somehow incredibly wonderful, that they had that memory together.

"Oh, it was awful. I cried. Jacob hid through most of it. It was hilarious."

"You two need help with the rest of the wreaths?" Jacob picked up two and took them inside the barn.

Charlotte shook her head. "Oh, no. I think we—"

"Lottie! Lottie, where *are* you?"

Jacob jogged back out of the barn, and he and Charlotte exchanged a look. "Mom."

Jacob nodded. "Okay, you go. I'll help Lars with the rest of the wreaths."

"Well I...um. Okay." Charlotte shrugged at her. "Sandwiches after?"

"And wine and chocolate mousse. The good stuff." She winked at Charlotte, trying to ease the worry. She wasn't going anywhere. Not at all. "But first, wreaths."

"Sounds great."

"Lottie!"

"Coming, Mom!" Charlotte jogged off toward the house, her boots kicking up snow as she went.

"So...you and Lottie, huh?" Jacob grinned at her and picked up a wreath with his good arm.

"Yeah. She's something else." And hotter than a firecracker on the Fourth of July.

"She lives in Denver, you know."

"I've heard that." But she wasn't in Denver now, was she? And she wasn't talking about going back and getting back to the fancy job.

"And she just got her heart broken." Jacob looked at her meaningfully. "Did she tell you?"

Nope, but she knew. One assumed, if they ever got to talk without a goddamn interruption, Charlotte might have time to tell her all about it. It might be next year, but... "Is this the 'stay away from my sister' talk, man?"

Jacob shrugged. "No. It's more like a...don't break her heart or I'll break your knees kind of thing." Jacob followed that with a wink and a grin. "I just care about her, that's all. I want to see her happy. And I like you, so...win-win?"

"I want to see her happy too." And the weird thing was? It was totally, unequivocally true. Lars liked Charlotte. She liked how Charlotte smelled, she liked the way that Charlotte understood steak and chocolate, she liked that Goober loved Charlotte. She loved the way Charlotte tasted like coffee and burnt sugar.

"Cool. Awesome. Because I'm pretty sure you can kick my ass even without the broken arm." Jacob clapped her on the shoulder in a brotherly way. "That one goes on the lamp post. You'll see the hook. I'm going to put this one on the front door. Meet you inside?"

"Totally." She stopped for a second, watching the three bassets play around in the snow. They were having a ball, ears flopping, huge feet slamming down and sending up puffs of snow. Damn, those babies were cute as anything. She chuckled, and that got Goober's attention, her goofy boy waddling over to give her some love. "Hey, baby. I'm hanging greenery."

Goober answered her with a little groan.

"You're right. I'd rather be hanging out with Char. Such a smart boy." She gave him a scritch behind one snowy ear and he thanked her by shaking all the snow off his coat.

They all headed back up to the door, and she knocked quietly, hoping Charlotte was waiting for her.

"Let's move to Bora Bora," a wide-eyed Charlotte said as she yanked the door open. "Like, now."

"Come on. I'll swing by and get the dogs." That was easy.

She wasn't sure where Bora Bora was, exactly, but she had Google on her phone.

"Never mind; they'd hate it there. It's hot." Charlotte looked exasperated. "Come in and pour me wine?" A warm hand slipped into her cold one and held tight as Charlotte pulled her into the kitchen.

"I can do that. Everything...everything okay?" Charlotte seemed at her wits end, and Lars wasn't totally sure why. Maybe she was just...that way. Lars was naturally a dork, so it could happen.

"Yes. Sorry. Mom is...she's upset about Dad and won't leave him alone, but she's also obsessed with this bazaar and has been asking all these questions about the details and who I'm calling and what still needs to be done, and if I screw this up I don't think she'll forgive me." Charlotte had turned pink in the face and the last few words were barely audible because she'd run out of air. She braced a hand on the counter and took a huge deep breath that would have been comical if she hadn't actually been trying to breathe.

"Oh, honey. That's not how family works. She's just stressed out." It had to be like if she'd hurt herself at the start of the season. She needed the money from the holidays to get her through the lean months. This place needed the bazaar. It was the way small business functioned, good or bad. "How can I help?"

That was one of Pappy's gems—when you didn't know what to do, ask what you *could* do.

"I just have to get it right. I have to." Charlotte leaned against the counter. "You have no idea the shit show I... I need to get *something* right. That's all. Why don't we start with the wine?"

"Wine it is. It's even a twist top because I'm classy like

that." She hadn't been sure if they were going to be in a place with a corkscrew. She even had Solo cups in her car.

Charlotte set out two jelly jars to fill with a grin. "Me too."

"Don't mind me, just passing through." Jacob pulled a sandwich and a beer from the fridge. "Thanks for dinner. I'm off to watch something on TV and eat and not be seen for a couple of hours. Mom and Dad have their door closed. So...that leaves you two the kitchen all to yourselves!" He gave a wave and took off, tripping over his own feet on the way out the door. "I'm fine," he called back as he disappeared.

Lars watched him leave with one eyebrow cocked. Jesus, that boy was a mess. Good thing he was basically harmless. "Graceful and delicate. I approve."

"Don't approve too much. He might break his other arm." Charlotte picked up her glass and swirled the wine in it, giving her goofy bedroom eyes. "What shall we do with the kitchen *all* to ourselves? Wash dishes? Ooh...maybe reorganize the potholders."

"I'm going to feed you chocolate mousse. Then, if you want, we can make gingerbread women."

"Oh...chocolate mousse?" Charlotte moaned, and Lars wished it wasn't just over mousse. She'd take it though. "Mmm. Yes, please."

"Grab a spoon. I brought the good stuff with chocolate curls and whipped cream." She knew from personal experience this was as close to sex that was legal in public.

Charlotte jumped up on the counter, then opened a drawer between her legs, eyes flashing. "Spoons are in here."

"Are they now?" That was an offer she couldn't resist. She marched right up, grabbed a spoon and then shut the drawer with her body, making sure to catch her free hand between Charlotte's thighs and her body. The spoon clinked on the counter as she pushed forward and braced herself as she lifted her face for a kiss.

"Hi." Charlotte picked right up where they'd left off in the barn, fingers diving into her hair and tongue pressing past her lips. That worked for Lars. She cupped Charlotte through her jeans, rubbing in time with the rhythm of Charlotte's tongue.

Fuck, she was melting.

"If we don't find some way to be alone soon, I'm going to explode." Charlotte sounded breathless as she rocked against Lars's fingers.

"Yes." She wasn't sure if that was the right response, but it didn't matter. Charlotte was right here, and she rubbed harder, wanting to hear more of those needy noises.

"I'm just grabbing some chips." That was Jacob coming into the fucking kitchen after saying they had it all to themselves. "Don't mind—oh. Oh! Crap."

Charlotte buried her face in Lars's hair. "Damn it, Jacob!"

"Sorry! Sorry. Oh my god. I'm so sorry."

Jacob disappeared faster than a roach when the lights came on.

Charlotte pushed her hand away and slid down off the counter. "Fuck."

"How disappointed would you be if I wrapped him in a wet sheet and beat him to death with a towel?" She felt like she was burning alive, and she wanted to grab Charlotte and take her home and keep her.

Goober started baying the second she spoke, calling for his mom.

"You might not need to, he's probably traumatized. Goober sounds lost." Charlotte picked up her wine and swallowed the whole thing down.

"Let me let him in to see me before someone smothers him." Lars opened the kitchen door. "Goob! I'm right here!"

Goober beat feet to her, sounding like a herd of elephants, ears slapping against each other. She knelt down, catching him.

"Poor little boy. Were you lost?"

Goober licked her hand and told her all about the snow and the other dogs. Charlotte brought a towel over for his feet and handed it to her.

"Oh, thank you." She caught Charlotte's hand, kissing her fingers. "You're good to my boy."

"He's sweet. And wet feet get chilly. I'll bring Jacob's pair in. Why don't we go eat by the wood stove in the den and they can all warm up?" Charlotte let Ginger and Bailey in and dried them off too. "Distract ourselves with puppies and wine."

"Sounds delicious." Not as delicious as Charlotte, but safer, and gave her another hour to learn about this fascinating lady.

"It's not everything I want right now, but it will do." Charlotte sent the dogs off to the den and Goober loped after them. Light fingers slid over her shoulder as Charlotte went to the fridge. "Thank you for dealing with the wreaths. I'd have lasted about thirty seconds on that ladder."

"No worries. It's my pleasure." And it gave her the chance to visit, so... "I'll bring the tree up a couple of days before the bazaar so you all can trim it."

"The big one? A week. We need it a week early. Mom says it takes that long to get the lights on and everything. Oh god, and that was Jacob's one job you know?" Charlotte sighed. "Tomorrow. I'll figure it out tomorrow."

"Then I'll bring it out a week early. Have you thought

about asking the band kids to come help decorate? Or the cheerleaders?" They seemed...decorate-y.

Charlotte's eyes lit up. "Brilliant. Again, you're brilliant. I'm totally doing that." She got a quick smooch, but Charlotte shook her head. "Sorry, let's not start that again. Sandwich?"

"Sandwich. Eating. Nom nom nom and stuff." Oh, that was classy. Of course, they were eating turkey subs.

"All right. Good. Yes." Charlotte handed her one, tucked one under her arm and picked up her wine and the bottle. "This is a picnic right? We don't need plates."

"Nope. We're being casual." Plates were overrated. Of course, they did have three shiny black noses, pointed at them, sniffing hard. "And if you drop anything, it'll get hoovered right up."

"You know it. Ginger. Bailey. Don't beg." When neither dog moved a muscle, Charlotte grinned. "That never works."

"No. No, they're hounds. They don't do commands where food is concerned." This she understood on a deep, personal level. She'd never had a single dropped piece of food since Goob came home.

"I can relate." Charlotte laughed and took a too-big bite of her sub, chewing in a goofy, exaggerated manner. Sure she wanted to get the woman alone, but sitting here, relaxed with the dogs by the warm wood stove she was...happy.

Lars guessed that was good enough for now.

Orgasms might be nice, though. Seriously.

9

Charlotte left Caffeine Ivy's with her latte and stood on the street in the sunshine looking at her to-do list on her phone. It was cold out, but it was nice in the sun, so she stood there a bit just breathing. Today was a good day, damn it.

Naomi had brought the tree over and was setting it up with her crew. Charlotte had hired a bunch of local kids to decorate it, so that was totally happening, and she was going to—

FERN:

Where are you? You weren't home. I'm headed into town.

The text notification popped up on her screen, obscuring her to-do list. But it was from Fern, and Fern lived in San Francisco and was *whoa* pregnant.

I'm at Caffeine Ivy's but what are you doing here?

FERN:

Cool. I just parked. Don't. Move.

Charlotte sipped her coffee and looked down the street in each direction, hoping to see her best friend. It had been forever.

Sure enough, Fern was coming down the street, belly covered in the biggest bright fuchsia sweater on earth, hair in long pink and purple braids. Whoa. "Lottie! Lottie, hey!"

"Oh my god. Fern!" She jogged toward Fern because she wasn't the pregnant one and went right in for a one-armed hug, holding her coffee out at arm's length in the other hand so it didn't spill. "I can't believe you're here!" She knew as soon as she got that hug that somehow this was all going to come together. Fern was here.

"I heard about your dad and Jacob from Mom, and I thought you could totally use a hand."

"I totally can, but you're a little pregnant, dork. Are you sure?"

"Troy is still deployed. Little Alicia is at her grandparents' getting spoiled rotten two weeks early. I am here for you."

Fern had that stubborn look and Charlotte knew there was no point in arguing with her. Not that she wanted to, she was getting desperate and everyone she knew was either recovering from something or busy. Even Naomi...this was her busiest time of year. Hell, Naomi ran a Christmas tree farm. It *was* her time of year, period.

She took Fern's arm and headed back toward the coffee shop. "I have so much to tell you. Do you want some coffee first? I forget—are you allowed to have coffee? Are you hungry? You wouldn't believe my to-do list today, and I have kids decorating the tree...that was Naomi's idea. She's brilliant." She stopped and took a breath. "I'm babbling. Sorry. I'm just so glad you're here."

"No coffee. Yes, hot chocolate. God yes, food. And OMG, I want to hear everything." Fern twined their arms together. "Let's go somewhere warm."

"Definitely. Nonna's? Cherry's?" Cherry's would probably have cocoa, and their pizza was the best in town.

"Cherry's! Pizza! God, have I mentioned my abiding love for pizza?"

"Alicia wanted tacos, I remember."

Fern chuckled. "She so did. This little girl? Pizza. All day, every day."

"It's like, second breakfast kind of hour, let's get your girl some pizza then." She and Fern didn't see each other very often in person, and it had been a while since the last time, but they always managed to pick right up like they'd never been apart. They walked arm in arm down the block and she hardly noticed the cold.

"So, we have so much to talk about. I feel like I've been missing you, your life." Fern leaned into her. "I mean, you know my life is fascinating—*Doc McStuffins* and *Paw Patrol*, *Sesame Street* and *90 Day Fiancé*. It's breathtaking."

Fern joked, but she knew Fern loved all of that. "And soon you'll have more endless laundry, diapers, bottles... you're going to be a regular party animal. When are you due again? Will Troy be home?"

"He won't, no. Just like Alicia." She sighed softly. "I'm due January eighteenth, but honestly, I feel closer."

"Well, whenever it is, I'll be there. Just like Alicia." She chuckled as they arrived at Cherry's and held the door open. "The way this bazaar is going, it might throw you into labor."

"Oh man. So, tell me everything. Do you have lists? What can I do? I'm here to help, all the way."

She pulled out Mom's planner and set it on the table. "My lists have lists. But Naomi is handling the tree today so we can cross that off at least."

"Naomi? Who's that?" Fern started looking through the planner, shaking her head. "Is she new?"

"Oh she's just...she's uh..." Charlotte felt the heat in her cheeks as she gave her best friend a sheepish grin. "She's new. And hot."

"Yeah? Hot is good. It's good that you're back on the wagon, right?" Fern had been there for her breakup with Rosalie, for the long, teary phone calls, for the new, little apartment.

"I didn't mean to get back on the wagon." She shrugged. "I don't know if I'm ready to be. But she's...more than just hot. I like her. She's interesting and fun." Naomi was here though, and she wasn't sure if she could come home for good.

"You can always use some fun, honey. You're so serious, so much pressure. Someone that can make you laugh is a plus."

The waitress came over, and Fern smiled at her. "Hey there! Do you have hot chocolate?"

"Only for pregnant ladies. You want food too? Or is this just a chocolate craving?"

"I want a sausage and onion pizza and whatever appetizer you have that involves cheese."

"Fried mac & cheese bites?"

"Perfect." Fern nodded and leaned back in her chair.

Charlotte laughed. "Well, okay then. I will have a slice of pepperoni, please. And a Coke?"

"You got it. Back in a jiffy." The waitress headed for the kitchen.

"You came hungry."

Fern rolled her eyes, oh so dramatic. "Starving. You know how my mother cooks. All chicken breasts and broccoli. I had to threaten her to get her to feed Alicia eggs for breakfast."

"What's wrong with eggs? She's crazy." The cocoa and her Coke came quickly, and she took a sip. "You see that list? It's insane. And Mom's handwriting is worse."

"Yeah. But we can do it. We'll just split it up. I can handle the schedule for the entertainment, if you want. And start poking everyone at the churches for the goodies for the cookie crawl. Maybe a craft table for the kids too—I bet one of the girl scout troops would do that." And just like that, Fern breathed life into this thing.

She stared at Fern. "God, I've missed you. I should have called you a week ago. If you could do that, I can finish up with the vendors and get the booths all set up."

"I so can! We'll have a ball. I love the idea of working together!" Fern took her hand, squeezed it.

"Maybe I'll even impress Naomi. I've been a basket case around her, she must think I'm a total spaz."

"If she likes you, who cares? Tell me all about her? Is she pretty?"

Naomi? *Pretty?* That wasn't the right term, not really.

"She's beautiful. She's tall and she's so strong, she has red hair and big brown eyes. She's a dogsledder, Fern. For real. She rescued me when my car died with her sled! She has a whole team of sled dogs and a basset hound named Goober." She was amazing, and the more Charlotte talked about her the more she wished Naomi was sitting there with them.

Fern laughed so loud that everyone turned to look and smile. "Dude! Dude, you're talking about the Christmas Tree lady! I met her last year. You chose a hottie."

"Right? Oh...you probably met her as Lars. Her real name is Naomi. And yeah, she's putting up the big tree at the farm right now."

"And you're here with me?" Fern's eyes filled with tears. "Oh, honey..."

"Whoa, easy preggers." She took Fern's hand. "You came into town for me! Of course I'm here with you. You're my bestie, and you came to save me. Drink your cocoa. Chocolate is good for hormones." That sounded good. It might even be true. Chocolate was good for everything else.

"Yeah. Sorry. I'm supersensitive girl right now. So, right. Activities. Entertainment. I'm your girl. I can put the announcement in the paper too."

Like magic, that sip of hot chocolate had done the trick.

She made a mental note to carry Kleenex and chocolate everywhere from now on. Fern had been supersensitive with Alicia too. Flowers had made her cry. Puppies had made her cry. So had dirty dishes, things she couldn't pick up off the floor, dinosaur movies, and anything having to do with the military. But pull out a Hershey Kiss or a mini Milky Way and all was right with the world.

"You're amazing." This was going to be great. She hoped that coming into town right now would be good for Fern too. It was something to concentrate on besides her impending due date and the fact that Troy had to miss this baby too. Charlotte had to pretend last time that she had everything under control on delivery day, and Fern had believed her. This time she actually had a little confidence. She'd done this before, and she'd be there for Fern again.

The case of very good wine that Troy had sent her after Alicia was born had been nice too.

The pizza arrived, and her stomach growled. She hadn't been hungry when they ordered, but she would have taken one for the team so Fern wasn't eating alone. The gooey cheese and sizzly pepperoni on her slice called to her as the waitress set it down on the table, and Fern's pizza followed, onions all caramelized and yummy looking. "Oh, yours smells so good."

"Right? There's just nothing like this combination right now. Thanks for indulging me." They set to eating, both of them chowing down and not chatting until post-pizza.

They still had the mac and cheese bites.

"So, what about the job in Denver, honey?" Fern asked as she wiped a bit of cheese off her bottom lip.

"What about it?" She went for casually curious, but it came out sounding defensive.

"Ooh, ouch. So, that's a tender spot. It can wait for wine and jammies and ice cream. I get it." Fern nodded, just like that was that. "So the bazaar—are you having food trucks?"

She sighed; she couldn't let that just go by. "You're good to me. So...yes. We're supposed to have food trucks. I was going to run around and confirm those today. I got a taco guy, a funnel cake guy, barbeque, burgers... I stayed away from the dessert places because we have vendor booths selling cakes and cookies and stuff."

"Cool. How about Cherry's? Are they selling slices or doing coupons this year?" They got into the nitty gritty of food and vendors and suddenly, somehow puzzle pieces started coming together. There was still too much to do and not enough time to do it, but one whole page of the lists was in Fern's hand, she had a dinner date to see her goddaughter, and she thought, maybe, she could accomplish this without having a screaming meltdown.

She might get a few minutes just to breathe and talk to Dad tonight.

It was even possible she could find a free hour to get busy with Noami.

But maybe she shouldn't jinx things. She should probably use that hour to figure out what the answer was to Fern's work question. What about that job? Did they want her? Did she want it? Did she even like Denver?

She liked the change of subject better.

"Alicia looks so tall in the pictures. She got Tony's genes, huh?"

"Obvi. She's going to be a basketball player or a supermodel or a super-tall scientist that has to order XL lab coats…"

"I'm going to call her Stretch." She sipped her Coke, and suddenly words just started pouring from her. "I totally blew it at work. I convinced a client that a marketing campaign that I really liked would work, and it didn't. I was way off. They were mad, my boss was mad, and it all went down a day before Jacob called to tell me Dad was in the hospital, and Mom needed help. I don't even know what's going on, they haven't contacted me. I might be fired. I did say I had a family emergency though, so… I don't know."

Fern stared at her, and Charlotte knew her best friend was pissed at her, disappointed in her. "Dude. Lottie. Your boss is an *asshole*! Who doesn't call to see what happened?"

She blinked at Fern. She'd assumed her boss hadn't called because she was good and fired. "I…well, I didn't look at it that way."

"That's just awful. Can you imagine? Someone you work with calls and says, 'I'm having an emergency,' and you don't find out what? If they need help? Nothing?" Fern's eyes flashed with righteous rage. "What an utter asshole!"

The little hairs stood up on the back of her neck, and she nodded. "You're right. What a total asshole. You are so right. That's just typical of those people, you know? Every man for himself, so competitive all the time, nobody cares as long as they get the next account." Maybe she'd just be done with that firm and get on with her life. "Who needs that bullshit?"

"Not you. You're smart and caring, and you are organized and a go-getter. You deserve to be in a situation where you're welcome and loved, dammit."

Loved might be a bit of a stretch but that didn't make Fern wrong. "I deserve better than being underappreciated and ignored, that's for sure. I'm not even happy there. I don't really care if they do fire me. I should quit first." She leaned closer to Fern. "I want this bazaar to be a grand, sparkling Christmas event that people are going to talk about for weeks. I want people to fight to get a booth next year. I want people to come to me asking for things."

So there, Toliver and Mulahey Marketing. *Take that.* She was going to show them.

"Right on, sister! Woohoo! Kick ass and take names!" Fern stood up, belly like a prow of a ship. "Guess what? My best friend Lottie here is running this year's Christmas bazaar, and it's going to rock!"

There was a shocked and silent pause while everyone stared at the crazy pregnant lady and, for an awful second, she thought they might get laughed out of the place. But then the room erupted in cheers. The bartender pumped his fist in the air. Someone bought them another round of chocolate and caffeine.

She wished Naomi were here to see this.

"Fern, you're a nut. I'm so embarrassed." But that voice in her head that talked to her like she was stupid was dead quiet, wasn't it? And she finally felt like she could do this. With some help from her hormonal bestie. Thank fuck for Fern.

"I'm your nut, and I'm your biggest fan, dorkwoman."

It was true. Fern had met her in sixth grade, had announced that they were going to be besties, and had never once faltered.

"I'm *your* biggest fan, nerdnugget." She stuck out her tongue like they'd been doing forever, and when Fern returned the gesture, they both laughed and got up. Well, she got up and then she helped preggers lever out of her chair. "Okay. I've got a couple of places to stop in town, but then I thought I'd head back to the house to make some calls before dinner. Do you need a ride? I'm driving Dad's truck. Can you believe it? That huge thing. I look like I'm twelve in the driver's seat, I can barely see over the steering wheel." She pulled on her coat and shook out the fuzzy hood.

"Nope. I am going to run home, kiss my daughter, and start making phone calls." Fern pulled her sweater down farther and patted her belly.

"Okay. Then I'll see you for dinner and some godgirl snuggles." They stepped out into the chilly sunshine. "You have no idea what all of this means to me. You being here, the pep talk...thank you."

"I'm so glad to see you, to help. I was so bored sitting at home." Fern squeezed her hand. "Tonight at six?"

"Six. Awesome. I'll have lots to report." She gave Fern a careful hug. "Thanks again!" She gave a wave and headed off with new resolve, wishing she'd worn her fancy boots to kick some ass in.

10

Lars stomped the snow off her boots before she opened the door to the M&M Outfitters, the bell ringing merrily.

Kylie Brockhurst was sitting there looking like a modern-day Amazon in North Face. "Dude, Lars. How goes?"

"Good. Good. You?"

"Eh, wishing it was summer, you know?"

Lars had to laugh, because Kylie was her total opposite. Kylie was a rafting guide and the new manager at the Outfitters, living for the summer, the river, and the heat. Lars felt most alive in the winter, running with her dogs, selling her little chunk of Christmas, and playing in the snow. Took all kinds. "I brought Liz and Lupe my schedule so y'all can book my trips."

She did a handful of dogsledding excursions for the tourists. It was a little money, fun, and gave the pups something to do.

"Oh yeah? They were just talking about you. It's good

somebody likes winter, right?" Kylie held her hand out for the schedule. "Have some coffee and warm up."

"Thanks. How goes?" She knew Kylie had a new lover, but the rumor was she was running things at the fancy hotel. "You going to be in town for the holidays?"

"Me and Britt are going up to my folks', and we're meeting her mom there." Kylie looked a little panicked around the edges.

"Whoa. Big stuff." That was serious.

Kylie puffed out a breath. "It'll be what it'll be, you know? Do you know Frankie Hoffman? She'll be here while I'm gone. Are you doing runs over the holidays?" Kylie looked down at her schedule.

"I'm taking off Christmas Eve and Christmas Day. Otherwise, I'll do four runs a week, two per team. Fourteen years old and up, with a signed form saying accidents happen." It was standard and true. "I can also do runs for Evie and Cheyenne's cabins, if they want."

"Oh, nice. We have that waiver. I'll adapt it for you. Do folks meet up near you, or here? I guess the runs are up your way, and the dogs so..." Kylie sat behind the desk, looking something up on the computer.

"I can haul over to the ranch or they can come to me. I only do the short rides with the kids at the bazaar. I don't like to stress the dogs." They were her friends, her family.

"Got it. I'll pass your schedule on to the bosses and set up the waiver tomorrow. I'm done for the day. You want to get a beer?"

"God yes." She wanted to sit and chill out for a few hours before she headed home to see the dogs and call Charlotte for a chat before bed. Between the bazaar, her high school best friend, and life, Lars hadn't laid eyes on Charlotte for a couple-three days.

"Cool. I've got my Jeep. I'll meet you where? Cherry's? Whitewater?"

"Whitewater works. I'll see you in a few." She waved and headed out. This was still a relatively quiet time in Summit Springs—a time where the bulk of the population was local. It wouldn't last long. After Christmas day, they'd start coming in again, pouring in through the summer and into fall.

That meant she could get a seat at the bar at Whitewater, and that she knew almost everyone there.

"Hey, Lars. What are you doing here? Is this busy tree buying time?" Paula had been behind the bar here for years. They'd gone to high school together.

"You know it. The kids are working their butts off. I'm scheduling for rides after the busy season. You been crazy?"

Paula handed her a bottle of Bud Light. "Yeah. It's good. I need the tips for the slow months." Paula leaned on the bar. "What brings you in? Are you meeting someone?"

"Kylie from the M&M."

She tilted her head. "Rumor is you're seeing Lottie Miller."

"Is that what folks are saying?" She wasn't going to deny it, but she'd let Charlotte be in charge of what everyone said.

"Stop it, girl. She's pretty. I bet you two sizzle."

"Wait, what?" Kylie came up behind her, hand on her shoulder. "Who are you sizzling with? What have I missed?"

"Lars and Lottie Miller." Paula's smile was wicked.

"Lottie, huh?" Kylie sat on the stool next to her.

"Belinda spilled the beans when she came by for her weekly protest of our grass-fed beef."

"Ah, Belinda. Did you tell her that soybeans used to be alive?" She grinned at Kylie. "I rescued her on dogsled. It made an impression."

"Oh? And you're not at all smug about that, are you?" Kylie grinned back slyly and picked up the beer Paula had just set down.

"Nope. I mean, seriously, how often does this happen? Damn rarely. I see her broken down. I rescue her. She's into me. And we literally ended up trapped overnight at my pappy's cabin."

Paula shook her head. "That is insane. It sounds like a story you made up."

"You got it on with fancy city girl Charlotte Miller in the cabin? She wasn't worried you'd smudge her makeup or wrinkle her silk blouse?"

"Maybe she wanted it smudged." Paula winked.

"She was wearing a sweater, no worries."

Kylie snorted over her beer. "So, she's in town because…"

"Her dad had a heart attack." Paula knew everything, or at least she thought she did.

"And Jacob broke his arm." Lars rolled her eyes. "She's helping her mother with the bazaar." Which was the main reason Lars hadn't seen Charlotte in days. Too many days.

"Oh, man. I hope her dad is okay. I'm sorry to hear that."

"He's home and recovering." And she was missing Charlotte something fierce. "Are you bringing your new lady to the bazaar?"

"Britt can't wait to come and see. It'll be her first bazaar."

"Charlotte's really trying to make it something special this year I think." She and her bestie seemed like a good team.

"Well, enjoy it while you can. She's a Denver girl now."

All Lars could do was make a noncommittal noise. That was between her and Charlotte. If Charlotte needed to be in Denver, Lars could visit.

Kylie waved her hand at Paula. "What do you know? She's here now, isn't she? Don't listen to her." Kylie turned her gaze to Lars. "Good things have a way of keeping people close."

"You should know, huh?" And that earned her a blush and a grin.

"Oh, man. I so know. She's a firecracker, and she stayed for me."

What could she say to that? If Charlotte asked her to go to Denver, she'd have to say no, so how could she expect Charlotte to stay in Summit Springs for her? They weren't there yet.

"Okay, so a whirlwind romantic rescue in a snowy cabin is one thing, but if you're still hanging out with her you must really like her, huh?"

"I do, yeah. She's funny, smart, and damn brave. She left a fancy job to come here and help her people, and she's handling the bazaar like a champ." At least she assumed so. No one appeared to be bitching about it.

"Does she like dogs?" Kylie teased.

"Her brother has two of Goober's litter mates. She had to sleep with the A team in the cabin..." She'd never once bitched about them.

"Sounds like you're a lucky woman. Can't wait to meet her. Or re-meet her. I'm sure I must know her." Paula gave her a wink. "And how are you otherwise? Tree business is good?"

"Exceptional. It's going to be a good year." She would save back a chunk to make it through a slow season, and then she'd buy a second sled.

"Oh good. It was busy here during the off-season, and it's been picking up steadily as winter sets in so I expect it will be a good one here too. Speaking of which, you folks want a burger or anything?" Paula grabbed a towel and wiped down the bar.

"Are you doing the Irish stew? I could go for a bowl of that before I head up the mountain." That would save her having to cook.

"You know it. Kylie?"

"Nothing for me, thanks." Kylie shrugged as Paula headed for the kitchen. "If Britt cooks, and I've eaten..."

"Hey, that's fair. I'd be pissed too." And she loved that Kylie cared enough to wait. Those sorts of things were important.

"Hello!" A giantly pregnant woman in snow boots and a warm, knit poncho half waddled, half marched up to the bar. "Hey, Paula. Nice to see you."

"Fern! Oh my god, look at you." Paula ran out from behind the bar. "Can I hug you? How do I hug you?"

"Sideways works." They exchanged a quick but hard hug.

"I'd heard you were back in town. You're not here to drink..."

"No. Nope. I'm here to beg a favor." Paula ducked back behind the bar and poured a glass of cranberry juice, which she sat on the bar for Fern. "Ooh. Cranberry."

"I remember that from your first. What do you need?" Paula asked, and Lars tried to pretend she wasn't eavesdropping.

Kylie wasn't pretending at all.

"Well, Lottie is doing a bunch of raffles at the bazaar, and we need some donations. Can I put you down for like, a couple bottles of wine, maybe a nice top-shelf scotch...some champagne?"

Fern was good at this. It was hard to say no.

This must be the very pregnant best friend. It had to be.

"Sure. Sure, I can donate a whiskey tasting and three wine and cheese packages. How's that?"

"That's perfect. You are the best." Fern hauled herself onto a bar stool and pulled a notebook from somewhere under her poncho. "Let me just write that down. I might put the whiskey tasting in the silent auction. What do you think?"

"Perfect. I'm happy to do that, honey."

Lars smiled over, unable to resist. "Excuse me, are you Charlotte's friend, Fern? I'm Lars. She and I met on her drive down."

"You're... Lars? Oh! So great to meet you." Fern stuck out her hand. "Rescued her from a breakdown, you mean. She's told me all about you."

Lars shook her hand and smiled. "All good, I hope. She's a special lady."

"The details fall under BFF privilege, but it's all good, honestly." Fern tilted her head, looking thoughtful. "It's weird... I know *who* you are—your business and your family—I'm surprised we've never met, but I've been living all over the place since I got married. Good to meet you now."

"I tend to be up in the mountains." She only really came down at this time of year and to resupply. Her life was very invested up on the farm. "And I'm a bit older than you, so we wouldn't have met in high school."

"Well, listen. I have to run. I've got a whole list of businesses to hit for Lottie. I'm sure we'll see each other again soon." Fern backed away a few steps. "Thanks again, Paula!"

"Any time, Fern. Looking forward to the bazaar."

"Me too! It's going to be the most fun! Ugly Christmas sweater parades and all!"

Lord have mercy, that little girl had an excess of personality.

Kylie, who had stayed interested but quiet, finally opened her mouth, grinning at her. "So, that's the best friend. You know she's getting on the phone right now, don't you?"

"Yeah." And didn't she want to be a fly on Fern's shoulder, hearing every word. "I would be."

"Who would you call?" Kylie asked, and Lars had a moment of this quiet, deep panic, because she wouldn't call. She'd tell her dogs.

She told her dogs everything.

Finally she settled on, "The first person that texted me, I guess."

"You don't have to call anyone; you have witnesses. Oh. Stew." Paula hurried to where one of the servers had set her stew on the bar and brought it over. "One Irish stew, and the bread is fresh."

"Guh. That smells like heaven. Thanks!" She offered the bread basket to Kylie, because no one should have to smell that and not have a bite.

"Oh, I like a girl who shares. Thank you." Kylie took a slice and inhaled. "Mmm."

"I'm a giver." She waggled her eyebrows.

"Ha! I'm sure your girlfriend appreciates that."

At this point, it was more "remembers it fondly," but Lars had hope. She needed to just go kidnap her lady from the bazaar for one night. Prove that they could have sex without a disaster.

"Speaking of which, I better get home to mine." Kylie got up and pulled on her coat. "Thanks for the company. We'll be in touch about your sled rides."

"Just holler. I'll be about." She waved and went back to her soup, texting Charlotte.

> Hey you. Having a good day?

CHARLOTTE:
> Is this that hot dogsledder?

She smiled at the quick reply.

> And studly lumberjack. Don't forget that part.

CHARLOTTE:
> Never. How's the tree business today, stud?

> Good. At the bar having soup. You?

She took another bite, trying not to spill on her phone or her sweater.

CHARLOTTE:
> Helping Dad with dinner. Then maybe I'll eat. Giving Mom a break to eat with Jacob. Just call me Charlotte Nightingale.

Poor baby. She had to be about to throw something at a window.

> Anything I can do?

CHARLOTTE:
> Fern has been super helpful with the bazaar. I'm actually excited about it now. But I miss your face. Send me a pic?

That was followed by a picture of Charlotte looking a

little tired, but smiling, the light catching her blue eyes just right.

She snapped a picture, noticing how her cheeks were bright red from the sun and the wind, and her hair was all over her head. It was her, all the way.

Charlotte tagged the picture with a heart emoji.

CHARLOTTE:
There's my lumberjack. That's some good blackmail material right there.

<3 Miss you.

She wanted to see Charlotte, just all of a sudden, so badly.

CHARLOTTE:
Breakfast tomorrow?

Yes. My place?

She could make pancakes and hide them away, let the kids mind the store.

CHARLOTTE:
Is that a good idea? I have so much work to do tomorrow.

Wink emoji. Sunglasses emoji.
Charlotte followed that with a fucking tongue emoji.

We could have supper instead. Spend the night together.

She wanted to try to actually have a second of naked time. Just like an hour.

CHARLOTTE:

Dare we actually plan that?

I'll pick you up at seven. We'll grab a pizza on the way up.

There. There was a plan. A good plan, even.

CHARLOTTE:

It's a date. I'll tell Fern. She'll hold back the flood waters for us.

Perfect. Go eat. I'm going to head out.

Was it too needy to tell Charlotte she could call tonight?

CHARLOTTE:

OK.

The little dots came up, then stopped, then started again.

CHARLOTTE:

I'm usually up late if you can't sleep.

Ditto. I can call when you get settled?

Her heart did a little jump and flutter.

CHARLOTTE:

Sounds good. Safe home.

She got a heart emoji.

Lars glanced up, catching Paula beaming at her.

"You've got it bad, girl."

"She's special." And that was that. Charlotte was special, worming right into her heart.

"I love romance at the holidays." Paula gave her a goofy look and batted her eyelashes.

"Shut up, woman." She slid over her credit card. "I need to drag my happy ass home."

Paula ran the card quickly and handed it back. "Happy tree selling."

"Thanks for the beer. Night all." She was whistling as she headed out the door. She had dogs to feed and a woman to talk to.

It was a solid plan. Especially with supper on the menu tomorrow.

11

Charlotte gave Jacob a hug at the top of the stairs. "Goodnight, bro."

"Night, Lottie. See you in the morning." Jacob disappeared through his bedroom door and closed it, and she looked around the quiet hallway and sighed. Mom and Dad were in bed, Jacob was in bed, the bassets were in bed... and the house was quiet. The first quiet moment she'd had all day.

She brushed her teeth and pulled on the big T-shirt that served as her PJ's, then texted Naomi. She'd been looking forward to this moment for hours.

> Finally alone. Tomorrow night is a full moon, you know.

Instead of the bing of a text, her phone began to ring, Lars's face popping up, and she answered with a smile. "Hello?"

"Hey, beautiful. How're you doing?"

She sighed. She didn't feel beautiful and she was super tired, but Naomi's voice felt like a warm blanket. "Hey, you.

Good. I'm good. I'm fine. Okay. Kinda tired." She puffed out a short laugh at herself. "Fern and I got a lot done today."

"I heard. I saw her at the bar. She's fixin' to pop, isn't she?" Naomi's laugh was soft, almost sweet. "What all did you do?"

"She's not due for a bit yet, but she thinks she'll be early. I was there for my goddaughter, and I'm planning to be there for this one, so I hope she at least hangs in until after the bazaar." She plopped on her bed and leaned back on the pillows. "Today she ran around—well, waddled around— and got people to volunteer things for the auctions." The silent auction and the raffles were big money makers for the farm, and they gave fifty percent of the proceeds to holiday charities also. "And I finished scheduling all the physical stuff—tables, booths, all the AV equipment and Santa's sled."

"Is Hank going to be Santa again this year?"

God, apparently Hank Stephens had been Santa for at least a decade. She needed to make sure Mom had called him. "I hope so. I really think it's going to be good, you know? Fern's got me all excited about it now. I can't believe she just showed up."

"That's cool. You said you've been friends forever. I mean, seriously. That's amazing." Goober woofed softly, and Naomi chuckled. "And you're my best friend, Goob. Always."

"Goober is the jealous type, huh?" That made her smile. She liked Goober. "And what did you do all day? Other than meet my bestie in a bar."

"Oh, same old same old. Wrangled kids and trees, made cocoa, delivered Christmas like the anti-Grinch." She could hear Naomi grin. "I put in my post-holiday schedule with the outfitters. That'll keep me busy for the slow bit of the winter."

"Oh, you do rides? How cool. I'd love to get another ride sometime...one that's not in a blizzard in the middle of the night."

"Anytime, honey. I do give rides—I have different packages. I'm careful with the dogs, of course, but they love their jobs."

"You're pretty incredible, you know that?" Naomi had her dogs, her farm, her business...she was her own boss, did her own thing. She seemed basically happy. Charlotte really didn't know anyone that was just...content the way Naomi seemed to be. Not even Fern.

"Me? Compared to you, I'm boring. You fascinate me. I could talk to you for hours, you know?"

Sure. Fascinating. Her. "Well, that's nice of you to say. I do like talking to you."

There was a pause, then, "Did I say something wrong?"

"No, no. I just—" *have a lot going on I haven't told you about and probably should.* "I'm tired. I don't feel interesting is all."

"Well, I think you are. So, what do you watch on TV when it's late, and you're tired?"

That was an easy one. She watched a lot of late-night TV. "I like the late-night talk shows. Jimmy Fallon, people like that. And if it's even later than that I watch cooking shows."

"I watch a lot of those. And weird-assed infomercials make me smile."

"I always feel like I want those things. Cooling pillows, fluorescent colored knife sets, weird non-stick frying pans that are probably toxic."

"Or the machines! Ovens that prepare, cook, and serve the chicken, then do the dishes and put the food away!"

She laughed, knowing exactly what Naomi was talking about. "Oh my god, yes. Gadgets galore! Oh, and Iron Chef.

It's always on in the middle of the night. Is Goober a night owl too, or are you on your own?"

"Oh, he loves anything that involves midnight snackage. Especially pepperoni. That's his favorite."

"I'll remember that. Always good to have the dog in your corner." She could just picture Naomi and Goober in bed, munching on pepperoni by the light of the television. Maybe she'd get to see it for herself tomorrow night. "I'm looking forward to tomorrow," she said carefully. Some part of her was sure she'd jinx them.

"I can't wait. I may bring you and the pizza up here, lock us in." So Naomi understood.

"Sounds perfect. I'll leave my phone in the kitchen." She exhaled hard. "We're due one night, aren't we?"

"We are. You're due one to just breathe and relax."

"That would be nice. It's weird. I'm looking forward to the bazaar. I think it's going to be fun once we're ready, but I also kind of wish it was over."

"Then what are you going to do?"

God, that was the question, wasn't it? What was she going to do? Her parents hadn't even dared to ask her that yet.

"Well, I have...a few options." Quit her job, leave Denver, move back here and...do something. She was practically decided. Fern was right; she wasn't happy there.

"One day you'll have to tell me all of them. I'm interested."

She snorted and shook her head. "Yeah. I probably should, huh?"

"Like I said, I'm interested. A lot. I mean, you've seen my life—dogs and trees. It's remarkably cyclical." Naomi's laughter was wry, but happy. "Not stable, but cyclical."

"I'm willing to bet there's more to your story than dogs

and trees." But dogs and trees worked for her. Naomi loved those dogs. She didn't even know what she had to show Naomi about her life. It felt like there was so little left of it.

"Maybe. Maybe there could be, right? I'd like to add to it."

"Mmm. Maybe." She grinned. "Let's see if we can make it through one whole night first."

Naomi laughed for her; the sound merry as hell. "Oh, we've already passed that hurdle. Let's see if we can handle one in my bed."

"I'm going to give it my best shot." She let her tone turn suggestive. "Promise."

"Oh, I hear that. I want to wear your ass out and make you want to...come again." The sultry words were ruined by the soft giggles. "God, I'm bad at this."

She snorted, trying not to laugh but it was hopeless. "Oh my god." She giggled madly and flopped over on the bed. "You really are."

"I know! Oh my god! You'd think that in this day and age I'd been all FaceTime and sexting girl, but no. Nope."

"No...no sexting. No. I can't even take a good selfie with my clothes *on*." Oh...photobooth. She forgot to make that call today. "Shit. Hang on. Just gotta..." she hauled out of bed, still giggling and scribbled a note for tomorrow in her notebook.

"Are you putting clothes on?" Naomi sounded confused as hell, but still tickled.

"Haha. No. Sorry. I needed to make a note to make a phone call tomorrow before I forgot." She flopped back on the bed with a sigh. "I need to write stuff down when I'm thinking about it."

"I understand that. I have a pad in the bathroom next to the shower."

"See? You understand. I just have too much going on to remember it all. And poor Fern, you should see her lists... she has preggo hormone brain and she writes things down more than once."

"Oh man. Seriously? That's scary to ponder. She was so sweet when we met her."

"She's family. Everyone that gets to know her likes her. She's just very real." Which she wasn't sure she could say about herself. At least not a couple of weeks ago. She was starting to think she might be getting closer now.

"That's great. She seems like a hoot."

"Do you have high school friends?" Or friends? Naomi seemed to know a ton of young people, but very few people their age.

She got a soft sigh. "No. I hung out with the other ranch kids, when I did. Pappy was getting up in age by then, and I had a lot to do. I spent time late at night online, talking to a ton of folks in the UK, in Australia."

So, her friends are all...in another time zone? "Well... have you been? To the UK or Australia? Do you want to go?"

"No. No, I went to Alaska to see the Iditarod. One day I'm going to enter. I've done a couple of the qualifiers, but that's it. It's an expensive sport."

"That's wild. Really? You totally should. You have to. That would be amazing." And scary, and dangerous, but still amazing. "I could never do anything like that."

"Well, you have to fly the dogs up, with enough handlers, plus supplies, entry fees, vet fees. It's an investment. The races here work for now."

"One day. It's a goal. You're going to do it. You can teach me to be a handler." She laughed. Imagine that? Being friends with all those pretty dogs.

"That's a deal. We'll have to go for a ride together in good weather soon. You didn't get the best experience."

"Oh no, it actually was the *best* experience ever." She'd like to teleport into Naomi's bedroom right this second and do it all again.

"Thank you. I will never forget it. Never. It was a fantasy."

"It was." She sighed. "I think I'm going to go to bed and dream about it."

"Tomorrow, we'll have a new night to dream about. Thanks for talking to me. I—it would be easy to get used to that."

She could get used to "Call anytime. I mean it. Any time you want. I won't even screen you." She grinned. She screened everyone but Fern...now Fern and Naomi.

"You too. You're in my favorites."

She liked being someone's favorite. She really didn't want to hang up; she could just sit here and listen to Naomi breathe over the phone, but it was late, and tomorrow was all about more errands for the bazaar. "Well... I can't wait to see you tomorrow. Sleep well."

"You too, honey. Night."

"Goodnight." She hung up and tossed the phone on her bed. One more sleep. This time tomorrow night she'd be feeding Goober pepperoni and snuggling with her girl.

12

_____

Lars headed across town with a hot pepperoni and green chile pie from Cherry's. She was supposed to pick Charlotte up at seven, and she wasn't going to be late, dammit.

There were a few flurries, but nothing to even notice. Just enough to make it pretty as she drove.

Which was great, because she was wearing a flannel shirt, jeans, and steel-toed boots, and she smelled like pine. Sort of intensely.

Cedar Ranch was all lit up. She passed the lamp posts at the end of the long driveaway, the ones she and Jacob had decorated with her wreaths, and headed toward the house, which had a warm glow spilling out of nearly every window and a Christmas tree with colored lights on the porch.

She pulled up in the circular drive, not totally sure whether she needed to park and go in or wait. Maybe she should text. But the front door opened, so she didn't have to. Charlotte stepped out in tall boots, dark leggings and her puffy parka with the fur-lined hood and waved, closing the door on two barking bassets.

"You made it." Charlotte shook the little dusting of snow off her hood before climbing into the truck. "Oh, it smells like pizza."

"Pepperoni and green chile. I got drinks at the house." She stole a quick kiss. "Let's get on the road."

The temptation to throw Charlotte's phone out the window was huge, but that would probably count as a mark in the weird-ass stalker column.

"Pretty night, huh?" A hand landed on her thigh and stayed there.

"Beautiful." She grinned, the pressure and heat of that touch like a dream. "How was your day?"

"It was crazy, but it went by fast. All I could think about was this. You." Charlotte glanced over, eyes twinkling in the dashboard light.

"Yeah. I changed my sheets and everything." Because Charlotte, somehow, was special.

Charlotte laughed, fingers squeezing her thigh. "Yeah? I put on pretty underwear."

Okay, that made her belly go tight, and she caught herself licking her lips. She hadn't been so deliberate about making love before. So sure that this was what both of them wanted. "I'm looking forward to unwrapping you."

"Me too. And I am a fan of pizza as a midnight snack. If Goober doesn't mind, of course."

"Goober doesn't get green chile. It makes him poop. I have a kid's sized no sauce pepperoni to share with him." Cherry and her cooks knew all about it.

"You buy Goober a special pizza? Wait until I tell Jacob."

"I do. I know. He can call Cherry's and ask for a Goob. They will totally understand."

"A Goob." Charlotte chuckled and leaned closer, and

Lars got a whiff of a light perfume. "Pretty drive in this weather."

"It is. I love this drive. Handy, since I do it all the time. It never ceases to make me happy though." They made the turn from the highway onto Beckett's Road, and she pointed at the light shining there. "My Pappy put Mr. Tumnus's lamp post up here for me, when I was eight, so I always knew my way back to Narnia."

"Aww. That is so sweet. He sounds like he was fun. Your mom's side or dad's?"

"My dad's. My mother left when I was a baby, and so I was raised by two of the most amazing men on earth." And she'd loved them both more than she could say. Pappy had read her *Heidi* when she was little, and she had been convinced that book had been about her, minus the goats. Pappy hadn't been fond of goats.

"Oh, wow. I'm sorry about your mom. But it sounds like you were just fine." Charlotte peered out the passenger window. "I can see why he put up that lamp post, it's dark here, huh?"

"Yeah. There's a little bench under the snow, too." There had been a playhouse too, but it had fallen down years ago.

"It's neat to live with all that history right? Family things. Our house is like that too. The farm has been in the family a long time. That's why Jacob and I are so determined to keep it."

"I don't blame you. It's a gorgeous place." Too close to town, too easily accessed by tourists, too up-scale for her. But utterly beautiful.

Charlotte nodded agreement. "I love how your house lights up the dark out here."

"Oh, I do too! It's just—I know it's silly, but I've lived here my entire life, and now that it's mine, I can make it what I want." She wasn't a girly girl, she knew, but there was a charm to her cabin now that had just been rustic before.

Charlotte pulled her seatbelt off as soon as she put the truck in park. "I like what I've seen of it. But I haven't seen the bedroom yet."

"That's the best part." The tree lot was closed, Vicky had fed the dogs, and so she grabbed the pizzas and her keys and led Charlotte up onto the porch. The house and office did look merry tonight, the tree in the window festive, the whole house lit.

"I have no doubt."

Goober met them at the door with his *sohappytoseeyoumomomg* doggy grin, ears flopping happily as he woofed at Charlotte.

"Hey, Goob! Who's a good boy? Did you miss your mom?" Charlotte bent and rubbed Goober's neck, gave his ears a tug. It was great that her girl was a dog person. That was kind of a requirement around her house.

She let him out to potty, stuck the pizzas in the toaster oven, then went to help her girl out of her coat. Her house was nice and warm; she didn't want anyone freezing to death.

"Thank you." Charlotte had on a sweater under her coat —a sweater *dress* that was all pretty cables and a cowl neck, she'd done her hair and was wearing eyeliner and pink lipstick. Charlotte bent and unzipped her tall boots, stepped out of them and set them by the door.

"You look so pretty." And she was a hot mess, but that was part and parcel of her job. "Let me hang up our coats."

She got the coats put away, her heavy boots off. "Would you like a glass of wine, honey? I'm going to have to get these work clothes off."

"If you have it, a beer is fine too." Charlotte took her

phone out of her purse and waggled it at her. "I'm shutting this off."

"Me too. I'll grab us both a beer." She let Goob in, locked the doors, then grabbed two Fat Tires. "Want to come upstairs?"

"Yes." Charlotte put her phone back in her purse and dropped it with her boots. "Finally. Yes."

"Good. Come on up." The stairs headed up to her room —it was a huge loft now, with her old room made into a sitting room and a great bathroom. If she had to live alone, she was going to enjoy it.

Her bedroom was all lodgepole pine, the heavy bedspread a deep purple and blue velvet. She had a chair up here, a gentleman's assistant to hold her morning's clothes, and there was Pappy's old, comfy sofa and chair in the sitting room with her books.

"You have a suite up here. Wow." Charlotte wandered the room, drawing her fingers along the velvet as she passed the bed. "It's so cozy."

"It is." And she loved the juxtaposition of heavy wood and soft and squishy bedding. "It's happy making."

She went to her en suite, leaving the bathroom door open as she stripped down to her undershirt and her jeans, washing her hands and face so that she didn't smell like sap.

Charlotte leaned in the doorway, watching shamelessly. "Scrub-a-dub-dub."

She chuckled, wiping off her face. "I didn't want you to think you were being seduced by Yukon Cornelius, honey. That would be...weird."

Funny, but weird.

"I don't know, he's kind of adorable in an animated way. You're much hotter, though. And he doesn't have your boobs." Charlotte backed out of the bathroom, eyes still on her.

"And I don't have his beard." She followed, eyes fastened on Charlotte. "Come here and kiss me, honey. I want you more than I want my next breath."

"Okay." Charlotte scrunched her dress up to her shoulders and pulled it off, then wiggled out of her leggings before stepping in closer. "I went shopping for our date."

Lars let herself admire, the matching bra and panties against pale, lush curves. Charlotte made her knees weak. She tugged her undershirt off, grateful that she didn't need to wear a bra under her heavy work clothes.

Charlotte took a quick, light kiss. "Beautiful." Chilly fingers slid across her cheek, then Charlotte drew her in, offering her more.

She wrapped her hands around Charlotte's ribs, thumbs drawing lazy circles as she pressed their mouths together, tongue sliding against the seam of her soft lips.

Charlotte tugged on her waistband, popping open the button of her jeans, and opened up, letting her tongue in, letting her explore. Charlotte tasted like mint and honey, like a sweet, hot herbal tea. It was the easiest thing on earth to sink into the kiss and let her hands explore the scalloped edge of that lacy bra.

"We can eat later, right?" Charlotte nipped her lip, then along her jaw toward her ear.

"Mmhmm..." She reached around to unfasten Charlotte's bra even if she was focused on tilting her head to expose more of her neck.

"Good." Charlotte nibbled and tasted her finally drawing an earlobe in between her teeth. A hand settled on her breast, thumb sliding over her nipple.

She felt jolts of electricity—all the way to her spine, and

her toes curled as she fumbled at the clasp. "Making me clumsy."

"There's no rush, baby," Charlotte whispered in her ear. "Just want you to feel good."

The air seemed to get heavier, and she sucked in a deep, deep breath. "You're winning there."

She managed to get Charlotte's bra unhooked, sighing softly as the weight of her breasts snuggled more firmly against her. Charlotte rolled her shoulders and let it slide off, then tossed it aside.

"I think we're tied." Charlotte kissed the end of her nose.

"Mmhmm." She moved to sit on the edge of her bed, humming deep in her chest as she nuzzled the soft skin of Charlotte's belly. Lars groaned at the scent of Charlotte, sweet and musky. "So pretty."

"All for you. This feels like a special occasion." Charlotte sounded a little breathless as she threaded fingers through Lars's hair, that composure slipping. "Finally alone with my lumberjack."

"You are." She rubbed her chin along the edge of Charlotte's panties, learning the softness, the smoothness of her skin.

"Mmm." Charlotte's fingers had warmed up and they slid over her shoulders lightly. "I'm counting on you to keep me from thinking about anything but you tonight."

She fully intended to keep Charlotte from thinking. Full stop. She licked the same line as her chin had taken, teasing and tasting.

The muscles there jumped under her tongue and sucked in a shaky breath. "That's a good start." Charlotte turned and sat on her knees, pulling her into another kiss.

Charlotte's body called to her hands, and Lars reached

up, cupping her breast and teasing her hard nipples, chuckling at the little jerks and shivers that earned her.

"Mm. Rough hands. So hot." Charlotte caught her lip between her teeth.

Lars grinned, waggling her eyebrows as she dragged her fingers in slow circles around Charlotte's nipples. She wanted until those perfect lips parted, then she tugged, just enough to Charlotte to really feel.

Charlotte gasped but didn't shy away from the pressure. "Fuck, yes. And what are you grinning at?" Charlotte returned the favor, rolling a nipple under her palm.

"I'm—" She leaned into the touch, her toes curling. "Fuck, that's good. More, honey."

"Lots more." Charlotte stood and pushed her back on the bed, dragging her jeans off as she moved toward the headboard.

Charlotte smiled at the little pinecone that was inked low on the curve of her belly, almost nestled by her hipbone. "I bet this was fun to get."

"Yeah." That was an understatement, but Mae hadn't been interested in Colorado and she wasn't staying in Idaho, so—

"Mm. That sounded loaded. We'll have to swap stories. Not now, though. I'm busy." Charlotte licked the ink and then nipped at it, teasing. "I missed this one in the cabin. I must have been distracted."

"It was dark." She arched a little, the motion instinctive and unavoidable. There was no denying how wet Charlotte made her, or how much she wanted to feel. "I like your version of busy."

Charlotte chuckled and twirled a finger in the waistband of her boy shorts. "This part I remember."

"Mmm...do you? I remember thinking I could die

happy." She lifted her hips in a clear offer, needing Charlotte to touch her, feel her, *something*.

"Hm. The lumberjack is out of patience." Charlotte teased and tugged at the waistband but finally slid her underwear off, then dropped kisses all the way back up her thighs.

She moaned, her muscles jumping and twitching as Charlotte's hair teased her, sliding over her skin. Fuck, her eyes wanted to close, but she needed to watch, to see this beautiful woman love on her.

Charlotte coaxed her legs open, not that it took any convincing, and the kisses continued along her thigh until a hot tongue dipped in for a taste. "This okay?"

"M-more than." Her belly had gone tight at that first, blistering touch, and she couldn't breathe as she waited for another.

"Mm. Hold on, baby," Charlotte whispered before pushing that tongue deeper and dragging it toward her clit. Lars could tell Charlotte enjoyed this—the attention was relentless and intense, the flicks with the tip of her tongue and the careful biting kisses were meant to make her wild.

Sounds began to escape her—little moans that were shaped like Charlotte's name, gasps that meant don't stop— and Lars fisted her hands in the sheets to keep herself from flying apart.

Charlotte's fingers touched her too, slippery with her own lubrication, circling and dipping gently inside her, just a little at a time. "Look at you, so damn hot." Char was breathless and her voice was rough. "I love feeling you move."

"I need you." She began to rock with Char's rhythm, her mouth doing dry as those fingers drove her crazy. "Fuck, honey. I'm going to lose my mind."

And she was grateful as hell for it.

Char moved up higher, lips finding her ribs, her breasts, fingers still moving in her, deeper and harder, thumb giving her pressure to rock into. "Yeah? You feel good?"

Good? She wasn't sure she possessed enough brain cells to answer even a one-syllable word, so she nodded, open-mouthed and eager.

"Mmm." Char hummed and sucked in a sensitive nipple, teeth closing in a firm bite as those fingers twisted just so inside her. Lars's entire body stiffened, and suddenly it was like a tightened spring let go inside her, leaving her shivering and riding a wave of pure pleasure.

Char let her ride the feeling for a while, kissing her breasts, her neck, staying close and warm. "Naomi. So gorgeous."

"Damn..." She sighed and then tilted Char's head, taking a long, thankful kiss. One hand tangled in the thick curls while she pushed the other down between them, cupping Charlotte through her pretty panties.

Charlotte moaned and leaned right into her, so ready. "Yes, baby."

She hooked her thumbs in Charlotte's panties, easing them down. "I want to watch you come, honey."

Charlotte lifted her hips to help, fingers tracing the colorful ink on her arms. "I'm all yours."

"Mmhmm..." She slid Char's panties off, taking a moment to admire the swell of Charlotte's hips, her sweet belly. "So fucking beautiful."

"It's nice to hear that. I like hearing you say it." Char's eyes were glued to hers, and those hips rolled, begging for attention.

She gave it, dragging her hand along Char's hip, the dark curls. Then Lars turned her wrist, sliding her fingers along

Charlotte's wet folds, making sure to nudge her clit as she did.

"Yes." Charlotte gasped and looked down between them, watching, and rocking into her hand. She was soaking wet, and Lars moaned as the heat coated her fingers.

She dragged her fingers alongside Charlotte's sensitive bundle of nerves, a long, slow caress.

"Fuck, don't tease, baby. I need you." Charlotte leaned in and covered her mouth in a hot kiss.

No teasing. She pressed two fingers inside Charlotte, using her thumb to work her clit, not letting up a bit.

Char's moan was muffled by their kiss for a second and then Char broke it off to gasp for air. Lars watched the look on her lover's face turn to pure need—brow furrowed, mouth open, cheeks blushing a beautiful pink.

"Show me, honey. I need it. I need to see you." She used her free hand to tug one nipple, nice and firm.

"Don't stop...don't...oh fuck." Char arched against her, hips bucking, eyes squeezing shut. When Char started to shake, those pretty eyes popped open again, searching until they found her face, and Char's fingers dug into her shoulders as she came in desperate, rolling waves.

Lars had never seen anything more beautiful, and she— god, she loved seeing it. She loved touching Charlotte.

She loved Charlotte.

"Fuck, baby." Char flopped on her back, breathing hard, pale skin standing out against her sheets. "You're incredible. That was everything."

She snuggled over, petting Charlotte's soft belly, cheek on one shoulder. "You feel so good."

"Mmm. Yes I do." Char laughed weakly. "Whoo. That was worth the wait." Char rolled up on one side, face to face with her in the pillows. "How about you? You feel good?"

"Jesus, woman. I feel—" Everything. "—amazing. That was—" Everything. "—perfect."

"Mhm. Yes." Charlotte played with her hair, tugging on it gently. "I think you should know I have a little thing for you, Naomi. A not so little, little thing."

Oh, thank god. "My thing is also way bigger than little, Charlotte. I love how we vibe."

"Me too, baby. I'm not sure you're ready for my personal brand of psycho, though."

"I'd love to give it a try. I'm not super-easy girl either." But she wanted to try. Maybe she needed to.

Char nodded. "We'll talk. I have...things going on. We'll snuggle with pizza and Goober, and you tell me yours, and I'll tell you mine."

"That's fair." She kissed Char's shoulder. "I've got beer and time."

"Mm. Beer. We had beer. Where did they go?" Charlotte grinned and kissed her. "Are you hungry? We have all night."

"I am. I'll run downstairs and heat it up." She stood, grabbing a sweatshirt that she used to keep her boobs from freezing. She thought it was a sexy look. Or at least she hoped so.

She wanted to make sure she gave Char incentive to stay.

13

Charlotte watched Naomi pull on a big sweatshirt, covering up that amazing ink and cute butt, and leaving just strong legs in view for a second before Naomi left the room.

She sat up and looked around, thinking about putting a couple of logs in the little pot-belly stove, but also thinking that she was toasty in this big bed with the heavy velvety comforter, and Naomi was already out of bed. She'd ask her lumberjack when she got back with the pizza.

She was eyeballing her beer over there on the little table by the easy chair too. Sex made her hungry. It used to drive Rosalie nuts.

But Naomi just hopped up and went to get her pizza.

What she needed to do was figure out some way to explain the last month or two of her life to Naomi without sounding like the nutjob basket case she was. Then again, she was exactly the nutcase she was the night she and Naomi met, so maybe that wasn't such a worry.

Naomi had always—from the very first moment— looked at Charlotte like she was magical, like there was no one that had ever been more desirable. It was crazy and wonderful and...just a little scary.

She wasn't magical at all. But that didn't stop her from enjoying every second of being looked at that way. Naomi's fingers *were* magical though. For real. Damn.

Naomi brought up two more beers in a bucket of snow, plus the pizza and paper towels. Perfect.

"Look at you! Do you need help?" She made a half-hearted move like she might get out of bed, which she would if Naomi needed her, but if not... "I was thinking about stoking your pot-belly stove too."

"I'll pop a couple logs in. I'm up." And when Naomi bent over to deal with it, it was worth staying in bed to watch.

"Your ass is perfect, you know that?" She pulled the snuggly duvet around her, eyes glued to her...lover? Girlfriend? "I love watching you move. You're so strong."

"Thank you. I'm trying." She got a glance over her shoulder, a wink.

"Trying to keep my eyes on you? It's working." Naomi didn't have to try very hard to keep her interest. Charlotte thought about her constantly.

"I'm glad." Naomi stood and stripped the shirt off, her short hair ending in a mess all over her head. She slid into the covers and pressed close a second. "Hey."

"Hey. Ooh. You're chilly." She put an arm around Naomi and rubbed her arm. "Better?"

"Yeah. I heated the pizza up and cooled the beer down."

She wasn't going to admit that her stomach was rumbling. Some people got sleepy after sex, some got shy, she got hungry. "Sounds great."

Naomi nodded and opened the box, the scent of tomatoes and basil and pepperoni spicy and delicious. "I brought paper towels. Is that cool?"

"Don't want sauce and cheese on your luscious, velvety bed." She kissed Naomi's cheek. "God, that smells so good." She was stalling a little, talking about pizza instead of her chaotic life. "Did you give Goob his snack too?"

"I did. I brought him a piece up here for later, but he isn't done going in and out the doggie door quite yet."

"Gotta patrol now that mom's home." She nodded. Jacob's pair were like that too. She took a bite and hummed approval, her mouthwatering as tangy sauce and rich cheese filled her mouth. "Mm. Good. Hungry."

"We got some exercise. It happens." Naomi took a piece and leaned back against the headboard. "It was amazing."

She nodded, watching Naomi, still sitting cross-legged under the covers. "My ex didn't like me eating in bed." As openings to awkward conversations went, that wasn't too awful.

"No? I have more than one set of sheets." Naomi gave her a wink. "How long were you two together?"

"Two years before she asked me to marry her. It was a short engagement." It was like Rosalie put a ring on her finger and it had turned her into someone else. She shrugged, not pretending to understand it. She didn't. "Just three months before Rosalie took the ring back and left."

"Just..." Naomi frowned and shook her head. "I—That is short. I mean, I've seen it happen, sure, but that had to hurt, bad."

She chewed her pizza and thought about how to answer that, determined not to let Rosalie ruin another moment for her. "It did. I thought I loved her, but things had been weird for a month or so and then she just...and I didn't get a lot of explanation, you know? I blamed myself for a while, I was sure I'd really fucked something up."

"I'm sorry. I mean...if you were married, I'd have missed

my shot, but I'm not an asshole enough to wish you pain." Naomi held her gaze. "I am glad you're free, though."

"Imagine if I'd married her? What a mess. I'm much better off. And I don't think I'm free, really. I'm...with you." She wasn't sure what that meant exactly, but she couldn't fathom walking away from Naomi.

"You are—both better off and with me, and I'm glad for it. I am into you, Charlotte. Like seriously."

Oh, god. She knew that, and she knew how she was feeling too, which somehow made this talk more stressful. "I know, baby. I was into you the second we got to your grandfather's cabin. I don't really have a name for it, but I understand now what Rosalie and I were missing. I want to spend every waking hour with you. I mean... I want to spend every sleeping hour with you too, not just the waking ones, but...you get what I mean."

Oh, good. Now she was babbling. Jesus, she was a gigantic dork.

"Yeah, exactly. It's like... I think about you first thing in the morning. I dream about you at night. I want to tell you about the cool things during my day." Naomi blushed dark, but the expression in her eyes was hopeful.

"Just like that." That blush made her smile and warmed her in a happy way. She didn't remember making anyone blush before. She tilted to one side and kissed Naomi on the cheek. "So. That's the Rosalie thing out of the way then. And for the record, I don't miss her. I maybe miss the ring though; it was sparkly and gorgeous." She winked at Naomi and chuckled. "Just a little."

"I can see that. You would wear sparkly and gorgeous well."

"I try." She chuckled and took another bite of pizza, polishing off her first slice. She put the crust back in the box, cleaned up a little with a paper towel and took another slice. "What about you? Newly single? Single for a while? Secretly having an affair?"

"I'm pretty much single. I had a thing with one of the vet techs about a year ago, but she was just in town for a few months, and she's in Vegas now, and she's dating a contortionist." Naomi rolled her eyes. "I mean, seriously, besides the long distance and the fact that we weren't mad about each other, who could compete with a contortionist?"

She rolled her eyes. That sounded fun but... "While I can definitely see the draw, a contortionist ain't got nothin' on a hot lumberjack with a fucking dogsled. Thankyouverymuch. You literally swept me off my feet. In the snow. In the dark."

"Got to love a woman that likes your dogs." Naomi's fingers tangled with hers for a second, squeezed. "And will eat pizza in bed with me."

"Dogs are okay, but the pizza thing is kind of a sign." She leaned back against the headboard alongside Naomi. "Gotta love her, huh?"

"Yes." There was no doubt, and Charlotte heard it, deep inside her. Wow.

Just...wow.

She should say "me too"—it was true, after all—but she was nervous. "If I think it but I don't actually say it, then I can't jinx anything. Right?"

Naomi chuckled softly, but she nodded. "I have to warn you, I'm steady and boring. Same job for my whole life. Same house. I'm not the type of woman that's going to ask you to go. Ever."

"I guess you think because I live in Denver that I'm not boring?" And there was the whole Denver issue. Did not asking her to go mean Naomi was asking her to stay? Why was she so bad at this?

She got a confused look. "No, I think you're not boring because you don't bore me. Do you like the city? Is it cool?"

"It's a great city. There's lots to do; there's great food, theater, all kinds of stuff." She chewed a bite of pizza thoughtfully. "But I'm not happy there. Everything that kept me there has fallen apart."

"Do you..." Naomi stopped, then glanced at her. "I don't want to sound pushy and stalkery and weird, but do you think you could be happy here?"

"Mhm. Right here. In this bed. Totally." She avoided the serious answer to that question because it was longer and complicated, even if it was still probably yes.

"Then we'll enjoy it, because you look right in this bed."

"I don't know if I still have a job. And if I do have it, I don't think I want it." She bit her lip for a second, remembering her conversation with Fern, then went on. "But what do I do if I don't have a job?"

"Get another one. Go into business for yourself. Do you like what you do?" Naomi actually seemed like the answer mattered to her.

"I like the idea of what I do. I don't like doing it at that firm. I don't really like the corporate...thing. Vibe. *Environment*. That's what they call it. The corporate environment is not for me." Go into business for herself... that was a great idea but...but. "I'd forgotten how much I missed this place though."

"Well, I know lots of folks do virtual work, right? You can work from wherever you want."

"So what you're saying is...you think I should stay?" She looked at Naomi from under her eyelids, flirting. Teasing. "Meaning here. In Summit Springs."

"I'd love it, if you stayed. Here." Naomi kissed the corner of her mouth, the touch featherlight.

She grinned, turning her head for a better kiss. "Was that pepperoni you were going after?"

"How did you guess?" Naomi's eyelashes were almost red, this close up.

"It's something I would do." She stared into Naomi's eyes for a long moment thinking maybe she'd be happy to stare into them forever. "Baby, you're beautiful."

Naomi's cheeks went bright red, and she glanced away before meeting Charlotte's eyes again. "I—thank you."

She took a kiss. The kind of kiss that isn't intended to lead to anything other than a smile. A real one. "You're welcome."

She knew how hard it was to accept a compliment without arguing, without denying it or just making justifications. She didn't do it very well herself.

"For the record? You're not boring. You're fascinating." She tried another quick kiss, looking for that smile.

"And we haven't even played poker yet." There it was— wide and happy and pleased.

"You think you can bluff around me, huh?" She didn't think for a second she could fool Naomi. Not for very long anyway. For someone who kept to herself so much, Naomi was very perceptive. She paid attention. Charlotte liked that. "We'll see. I'm a bit of a card shark."

"Yeah? Good to know. Kylie and Evie and Dr. Amy come up once a month or so for poker night. You'll have to sit next to me."

"You might peek at my cards." She tossed her second pizza crust into the box. "That was perfect."

"Might? Might? I will use whatever benefits I have at my

disposal!" Naomi was cracking up, snapping up the last of her pizza, crust and all.

"Hand me my beer, you dork. And tell me something that will make me feel less of a hot mess."

Naomi handed over the bottle. "Everyone seems crazy excited about the bazaar?"

Oh. That was good to hear. "Really? You think so?"

"I'm really starting to hear about it when I head to town. They're all ready. There are flyers in the hotel and at the diner."

"That was Fern. She made the flyers for me. She really lit a fire under my ass, you know? But do whatever spiritual thing you do and ask that she not go into labor before Christmas. She's as big as a house."

"Is her husband going to be able to come home for it?"

"Oh, no. He's deployed. He was deployed when Alicia was born too. I'm the swing." She rolled her eyes. "I'm enjoying having kids vicariously through my bestie."

"You're a good best friend." Naomi grinned at her, one finger dragging down along her belly. "Do you think you'll ever want kids?"

She bit her lip and tried to figure out how to answer that. She knew the answer, but it seemed like nobody ever liked to hear it. "Not really?"

"No? I have a lot of kids around working. I love them, but I don't have to raise them, just hire them." That didn't sound upset, just a fact.

"I've got Fern's kids. I can babysit. Are you...you don't want kids?"

"I have a job that involves axes, needy dogs, and a house with steep stairs. My life is not babyproof."

"Oh my god." She lost it, giggling madly, leaning into Naomi. "I'm so sick of people giving me that look, like I'm a horrible human being because I don't want to chase a toddler around."

"If you change your mind, I'll grab you a puppy to chase. It'll cure you in seconds."

That was all it took before she cracked up, laughing so hard that they bounced on the mattress.

"I don't have to cook for puppies! And puppies can sleep in the barn with their own parents. Puppies don't wear diapers or have homework." She shook her head. She was so fucking relieved. She couldn't wait to tell Fern.

"They have accidents, training, and they are trouble!" Naomi's giggles filled the room. "But you don't pay to send them to college, do you?"

"They don't talk back. And they stay cute." She took Naomi's hands. "I am so glad we are on the same page here."

"Well, that's why I asked. It's important to know who you are, huh?"

"Yes, and I know. But my parents aren't thrilled, and everyone always acts so shocked. Like I'll change my mind one day." She looked at Naomi seriously. "I'm not going to change my mind."

"Jacob will pump out six hundred babies. They'll be fine." Naomi's voice was serious, but her eyebrows gyrated wildly.

"He and his cosplay girlfriend. Can you cosplay babies?" She chuckled. It was true though. Jacob would eventually have enough kids for both of them. "He'll be a great dad too."

"You can cosplay with your babies..." Naomi sipped her beer. "So what's left to do before Friday's tree lighting?"

"Oh, no. I need to have sex with you three or four more times before talking about the bazaar again." She closed the pizza box and looked around, then slid out of bed and set it on the bathroom counter to keep it safe from Goober. "At least."

"I do love your priorities, honey. Seriously." Naomi snagged her as she got back to the bed. "C'mere, woman."

Her lover was shockingly strong, and Charlotte came flying into the bed. Okay, that was hot. She shrieked playfully and put her arms around Naomi's neck. "You brute! I love it."

"That's me, the brutish wonder lumberjack!" Naomi smacked her with a happy kiss. "Beware of my chopping ability!"

She blinked at Naomi. "I don't even... I have no smartass comeback. I'm speechless." She laughed and rolled, pulling Naomi with her. "But I have the element of surprise!"

"Jesus, you make me happy." Naomi straddled her, kissing her good and hard. It wasn't the kiss that stunned her, though. It was the pure joy in Naomi's voice.

The kiss left her breathing hard. "Yeah? I'm happy too. There might be a way you could make me a little happier." She licked her lips. "Just a little."

"Why, Miss Miller! Are you coming on to me?"

Hell yes. Yes, she was. "What was your first clue? My flirty smile, or being completely naked in your bed?"

"Hmm..." Naomi tossed the comforter over them and started slipping down. "Let me get right back to you..."

"No rush. No...rush." She wasn't going anywhere.

Well, except to the moon and back. *Damn.*

14

This had been a huge year for sales, and Lars was having to cut more trees to keep up with demand. She didn't mind it—she wasn't running lean, and in her heart she knew she was more invested in keeping the forest full than making pennies—but this was the last batch. Once these last few trees were harvested, that was it.

Merry goddamn Christmas.

"Come on, Draven. Move your ass." She was cold, hungry, and she wanted to get downtown, deliver her trees, and meet Char for lunch.

She waited for her eternally late employee to grab the chainsaw.

"Sorry, boss." Draven came loping up through the snow, hauling a chainsaw in one hand and gloves in the other. "I just had a...thing. You know. Dad. And then the truck didn't start. Sorry."

"I know. I know. Come on, man. I want to get a dozen more. You can handle that, right?"

"Yes, ma'am. I'm on it." That was Draven; getting him there was a bit of a challenge, when he was present, he worked hard. "I heard we're in for more snow, huh?" Draven followed along behind her.

"Yeah, they say it's going to be a hell of a winter. I'll be up here training with the dogs." And hopefully learning more about Charlotte. Like whether she drank tea after supper and her position on checkers.

"I keep trying to learn snow biking, man, but there's too much fresh powder on the trails. I guess I'm gonna have to ski instead."

"Oh, the humanity," she teased, feeling like she could. She'd known Draven forever. "Go get your board and ride. I know you love it."

"Yeah, yeah. I can totally board. I just want to try something new. I'm saving up for a snowmobile too." Draven was an outdoorsy kid. Other kids might talk about school, or bands, or something they were reading, but with this kid it was always about what he was doing outside. And football, the kid knew his football.

"That's an expensive hobby, but fun. Damn." She grinned over. She knew about expensive hobbies and snowmobiles. She had two old power sleds in the shed for when the dogs weren't wanting to train.

"So, are you getting any new dogs this spring?" Draven stopped by a nice-looking tree.

"I don't think so. It'll be a couple of years before I need to update the team." She wasn't ready for puppies. Not yet.

"Yeah. You got your hands full." Draven pointed. "This one?"

She looked around, judging distance and size and all, then she nodded. "That works. I want it to fall uphill, okay? I don't want to go chasing it."

"Okay. So you want to cut over here, and it'll go that way. Right?" Another year and Draven would be able to do this himself. Not that he wasn't capable, but the last thing she needed was for the little shit to cut one of his legs off.

"In theory. Yes." And god knew she'd done it enough that she ought to not screw it up.

"In theory." Draven grinned. "You cut. I'll load the trailer."

"You know it." She started the chainsaw, and got to work, cutting the first tree without a problem before she headed to cut the second.

"One down." Draven dragged that tree off, tossed it on the trailer, and came back for number two.

Together they got ten trees cut and loaded before she decided to call it. That was enough, she was tired, and she wasn't interested in—

Whoa.

That was a gorgeous tree—full and green, symmetrical and lush—and would sell for a pretty penny.

Dammit.

"Let's go ahead and get this one."

Draven laughed and stepped out of the way. "Just one more, huh?"

"Just one more. This is a beaut."

"Greedy!"

"Not so. I have a dozen mouths to feed. Toothy mouths. Have you seen my packs?" They liked their food.

"And Goober, who eats like he's a dozen."

"Maybe two. He's unique." In all things and in all ways. Goober was her baby. "Okay, let's do this."

She started the saw and got to work, the metal tearing through the wood like butter, at least until it didn't.

"What's up?" Draven shouted at her, moving in her direction. "Are you stuck?"

"No, just thought I'd take a second's rest! Get back!" Of course she was fucking stuck.

Draven stepped back as he was told, but that didn't change her predicament at all. "You want me to get the axe?"

Oh, smart boy. She'd taught him that trick. "Maybe." She gave it one more try and the saw slipped free, but it kicked back unexpectedly. And hard. The chain brake worked great, but her ass was in the snow.

"Shit! Lars! Boss! You cool?"

"Yeah." She tried to bring her arm up and it screamed, all the way from fingers to the top of her head.

"You don't look cool. You look white as the snow." Draven shut the saw off and moved it aside. "Can you get up?" He offered her a hand.

She took his hand with her other hand, and he winced for her.

"Not the shoulder."

Lars nodded and pondered whether puking would make the kid respect her less. "The shoulder."

"Okay. Okay. You need to get in the truck. I'll turn on the heat, and then I'll get this tree down, and then we'll...well, just get in the truck first. Can you walk?"

"Yeah. Yeah, I can. I got this." Once she was upright, she felt like she could manage, and she made it to the truck. Draven could drive them down.

Draven ended up helping her get in and pulled her seatbelt across for her. He started the truck and cranked the heat, and she watched as he put his foot against the tree trunk and kicked it over. It didn't take him long to load the tree, but she was really hurting by then.

"So... Smiths' Clinic? Are they open? Or just urgent care?" Draven put the truck in gear, handling it and the trailer well. "Guess we should ditch your truck and take mine."

"Just urgent care. It's not serious." She hoped. She needed it to not be serious, for fuck's sake.

"If you say so." Draven didn't ask questions; he just drove to the tree farm where his truck was and parked the trailer. He beeped the horn twice, and Vicky came jogging out of the sales hut.

"Dude, what happened?"

"Knot in the tree. No blood. Shoulder."

"Ah. So urgent care, not 911." Vicky peered at her. "Yeah, definitely urgent care."

"Can you help get the Boss to my truck? I'll lock up these keys."

"Yeah. You want me to come with you guys or I can go feed the dogs and stuff."

"Take care of my guys, please. Please." She knew she wasn't going to just be able to hurry home. Doctors took forever.

"No worries." Vicky helped her move to Draven's truck, which was sketchy, but it wasn't pulling a trailer full of Christmas trees. She knew Vicky could handle it; she just needed to get this fixed and get home.

She grabbed her phone and texted Charlotte.

> Can't make supper. Call 2nite

It was the best she could manage.

CHARLOTTE:

> Shit, really? Why does the Universe hate us? Miss you.

> u2. call l8tr

God, she was hurting, her right side a story of pain and heaviness.

Draven drove them to urgent care, and she appreciated that he was good in the snow. He drove just fast enough to be in a hurry but not so fast they ended up in a ditch. He hopped out when they got there and opened up her door for her.

"You're looking pretty pale, boss. You want a...like, a wheelchair or something?"

"Don't be a dork, man. I could cut off a limb and walk in." She might have to lean some, but she could manage it.

"I bet you could." He helped her out and locked up his truck.

Lars made it all the way into the line before someone stepped back into her and bumped her hard enough that the world went bright white, then black as pitch.

15

Fern.

Mayday Mayday Mayday.

Santa broke his leg skiing.

I don't have a Santa for the opening
ceremony tomorrow.

Repeat! NO SANTA.

Call me.

Charlotte left the house, balancing her phone with her planner, her pocketbook, her sunglasses and a cup of coffee. She had four thousand errands to run, food to pick up and now this call from Aaron saying that his dad had broken his fucking leg and was in the fucking hospital after fucking surgery.

Fuck.

And all her mom kept saying was, "Well, what are we going to do now?"

We...meaning Charlotte. That didn't take a genius.

Fern was probably still sleeping too.

And why didn't Naomi call her last night? It would be way better to be having this nervous breakdown in Naomi's bed.

She stopped next to her dad's truck and stared at it.

Right. Keys. Fuck.

They were in her pocket.

Okay.

She tucked her phone in her pocket, the planner under her arm, stuck her sunglasses on her face, then reached into her pocket for her keys...and dropped her coffee in the snow.

"Goddammit! Dammit." She groaned and bent to pick it up and the pocketbook slipped, knocking the keys out of her hand and into the snow too. She growled and straightened up, and just as she was about to hurl the fucking planner in frustration she stopped herself and clutched the book to her chest.

"No, Charlotte. No no. Nope. Down girl. The book you need. You can burn it in a week, but today it's a bible."

Jesus, she was breathing like she'd run a marathon.

She took a deep breath and puffed it out. And then another. And one more because why not?

Of course, on breath number three, Aunt Deenie's ridiculous lime green and pink smart car with silver eyelashes on the headlights pulled up, stopping right next to her and covering the keys up. "Did you hear about Hank Stephens? He broke his leg? Who's going to be Santa? Pappy Beckett's dead!"

Rule number one, don't ask for Deenie's help.

"I know, Aunt Deenie. Aaron called me. I've got it under control."

Liar. That little voice in her head that liked to point out how stupid she was taunted her.

She mentally slapped that asshole in the face.

"Are you going in to check on Mom?"

"Of course. And I'm meeting some people here to talk about the main stage. Fern called me this morning because I told her I was at loose ends."

She was going to show someone loose ends.

"Loose...oh never mind. I'll talk to Fern. Could you back your car up a foot or so please?" The coffee she could rescue. Her keys were literally under Deenie's tire.

"Sure, honey. I made you pecan rolls for breakfast, and I have an amethyst to calm your day." Deenie backed the car up about an inch. "More?"

"More!" She could take or leave the rocks, but oh...pecan rolls sounded good, and knowing Deenie, they were right out of the oven. "Yep, more please!"

Deenie finally got it right, then gave her hot rolls, traded coffee cups with her, and handed her a purple stone bracelet. "There. Better. Did you hear that Lars Beckett was in the ER last night? Ambulance came and everything. Quite the drama."

"What?" She almost dropped her coffee again. "What? Ambulance?" She had to call Naomi now too. She trudged back toward the house balancing everything awkwardly again, with added warm rolls she had zero intention of dropping.

She'd sacrifice her planner first. She so would.

She got her and Deenie inside, then took food and coffee upstairs to her room so she could shut her door against the family and eavesdroppers.

Still no text from Fern, she noted as she dialed Naomi

and stuffed a bite of sticky pecan roll into her mouth while she listened to the phone ring.

Finally Naomi's voice sounded, dazed and rough. "'lo? Char?"

"Mm. Mhm." She chewed quickly but the bite was sticky and wasn't going down. "It's me," she said with her mouth full. "Eating, sorry. Why does my Aunt Deenie know that you were in the ER last night and I don't?"

"Huh? Deenie's the biggest gossip on earth? Was puking. Pain pills. Vicky stayed to help with the pups. Miss you."

"Pain pills for what? I'm coming over." She stuffed another huge bite in her mouth and slid off her bed. Fuck Santa.

"Dislocated my shoulder. 'm okay. Sore."

"Charlotte? Honey? You have a guest!" Mom sounded...confused.

"Jesus. Hang on." Stress eating was not making this day any better. She opened her bedroom door. "What? Aunt Deenie is here to see you, Mom!"

"No, this is a—Mrs. Edmond? Oh, sorry, *Ms.* Edmond."

Her boss? Seriously? Here?

"What the fu—I mean...tell her I'll be right down." Her head was spinning. She put the call on speaker and dropped her phone on the bed. "Naomi? Are you sure you're okay? That sounds bad." She brushed the breakfast crumbs off her cleavage and checked herself out in the mirror.

"Just sore. I know you're busy with the bazaar. I'll try to come down this afternoon, maybe."

"You rest. Santa broke his leg, I'm covered in sticky bun, and my boss just showed up at my door. I've got plenty to keep me busy."

This was her fucking life. This was it. Not the calm, quiet of Naomi's life...no, this was her lot. Chaos and sticky buns.

"What happened to Hank? Your boss? Sticky bun covered Charlotte is a wet dream..."

God save her from cute, goofy lumberjacks.

"You're on some good drugs, baby." She chuckled as she changed her shirt. "Hank broke his leg skiing. Why is my boss here though?" To fire her officially in person? That seemed ridiculous. That's what Zoom was for.

Or even texting.

"She's going to beg you to come back. Remember that I love you and have your back, no matter what."

No matter what. She understood what Naomi wasn't saying, but they'd said it all the other night. "Don't worry. The only reason I'll going back to Denver is to move out of my apartment. I'm staying."

"I'll help. You can show me around. Call me if you need me, honey."

"I will. I feel awful that I can't be there right now. I'll come soon. You get some rest." She paused a second and then added, "I love you."

"I love you, Char. I got you."

They hung up, and she smoothed her shirt over her belly and hips. God.

One more check in the mirror and she turned and marched downstairs, leaving all the food behind. She'd come back up and eat it all after Harmony left.

She headed into the living room where she heard voices, suddenly realizing with horror that both Deenie and Mom were talking Harmony's ear off. "Hey. Sorry to keep you waiting."

Harmony stood, dressed to the nines — like she was attending a board meeting in Denver and not on a farm in Summit Springs. "No problem. I tried to call, but I didn't have signal."

"It can be weird." Especially if you didn't have the one and only carrier that really worked in Summit Springs. She looked at Mom and Aunt Deenie and gave them the you-can-go-now stare. "Thanks for entertaining her, guys."

Deenie nodded and didn't move. "It's no trouble. We're very friendly here."

"Deenie. I need some help in the kitchen."

"I think Jacob is in there."

Mom gave her aunt a look. "Deenie."

"Oh! Oh my goodness, we have so much to do in the kitchen," Deenie said, exaggerating her words like she was talking to Granny after she'd gone deaf. "It was nice meeting you, but we have to go now. So much to do. Bye bye!" Deenie just kept talking as Mom dragged her away.

Harmony arched one, perfectly drawn in eyebrow. "They're both charming. I can see where you get your sense of humor."

"I'll take that as a compliment." She was pretty sure it wasn't. "So what in the world are you doing in Summit Springs?"

"I was shopping in Aspen, and I thought I'd see where my errant employee was, and whether I could help with the 'family emergency'." She put air quotes around the final two words.

What the actual...?

"Okay, so... I'm not your 'errant employee'," she air quoted back. "I'm not 'errant' at all. Have you seen my dad around? No. You know why? Because he had a heart attack, and it's his nap time so he's upstairs resting. And you know what else? My girlfriend was in the *ER* last night, and my very pregnant best friend whose husband is *deployed*, thankyouverymuch, isn't answering my texts. Oh! And Santa broke his goddamn leg! I'm not 'errant'. I'm stressed and overwhelmed, and I hope you bought something nice in Aspen!"

Whoa.

Whoa, okay. That was maybe a bit much.

Somewhere in the back of her mind someone was applauding.

Or maybe that was real...

Fern stood there, wearing a bright pink and turquoise polka-dotted sweater that stretched over her gigantic belly, pigtails, a silver sparkly light-up hat, and red glitter Ugg boots, beaming and clapping for her.

Harmony, on the other hand, was possibly going to have a stroke.

She took a deep breath, let it out slowly, and in a measured tone she said, "And I quit."

"Cool! I have a bead on a new Santa and he has a Great Dane that will wear reindeer antlers!" Fern was beaming to beat the band.

"You quit? For what? A small-town festival with—" Harmony glanced at Fern. "—questionable taste levels."

"Oh, fuck off, bitch. Our taste levels aren't questionable in the least. We're *stunning*!" Fern just beamed at Charlotte, and Aunt Deenie bustled right back in, almost knocking Fern over with her breasts.

"You're disturbing my girls, Aspen. Get out."

She ran for the door and opened it. "You came all the way here for a fight, Harmony, and you lost. Enjoy Aspen. I have to find antlers for a Great Dane."

"You're even more insane than I thought you were. I'll have payroll call you." Harmony marched out of the house.

Ginger and Bailey came bounding over from the side yard, barking and kicking up snow, and she just shut the door. "I hope they eat her."

"If nothing else, they'll drool on her shoes." Fern's grin was positively evil. "That's a fate worse than death."

She ran to Fern and hugged her...kind of sideways to avoid the belly. "You are my glitter-glam guardian angel."

"I try. Why on earth is Naomi in the hospital, and do you need to go to her? I can handle Santa with Aunt Deenie."

"I...even without Santa I have so much to do. I'll see her tonight. Fern..." She collapsed in a chair. "Aunt Deenie... I just quit my job."

"You didn't have one when you got that one." Her Aunt Deenie walked behind the chair, rubbing her shoulders.

"No, but I had a fancy degree and a lot of confidence. And I wanted to—" Not be here. She'd wanted to be anywhere but here. Now here was the only place she wanted to be. "I was motivated."

"And now you have a fancy degree and experience. And a supportive family."

"And friends," Fern added.

Mom chuckled and handed her a mug of tea with honey. "And a girlfriend. Lars, I assume? She's always been so kind to us."

"Maybe. Yes." She hid her blush in her tea and took a sip before answering. "I am a hot mess. Hopefully Na—Lars can handle it." Naomi could handle it; she was pretty sure Naomi was the only one who knew exactly how to handle her.

She looked at Fern, ready to get her head back in this bazaar thing. "So. Tell me all about Santa."

16

T he texts from Charlotte had been...wild. Seriously wild.

CHARLOTTE:

N, I quit my job

I found santa

I need a beer

do you know a belly dancing troupe?

Can your dogs bark jingle bells?

I'm bringing tacos

Did I mention I quit?

Somewhere Lars had lost the thread, but she managed to answer with.

I like tacos. And you. I love you.

Her phone rang about twenty minutes later, Charlotte's name popping up.

"Hey, you. Where are you?"

"Stuck at the end of your driveway with your moose friend. Just...waiting for him to move. This is like, the cherry on the melted sundae of my day."

"Oh. Well...just don't honk. He'll move on." She hoped.

"Don't tell him I have tacos. She'll be jealous. How are you doing?"

"Sore as hell, but I'm getting better. I don't like this sling thing." She was already tired of it.

"How long do you have to—oh good Miss Moose is moving—how long do you have to wear it?" She could hear the car's engine rev as Char started moving. "Bye, moose!"

"They say six to eight weeks." If it made it through tomorrow, it would be a damn miracle. She had work to do, and her work truck was a standard.

Char snorted. "Oh, sure. Whoever told you that clearly doesn't know you. I'm hanging up now. Let me in. I have tacos and kisses."

"Coming." She wasn't looking her best. She had on a sweatshirt and the oldest pair of shorts on earth. Vicky had brushed her hair for her, so at least that was a thing.

When she opened the door, Charlotte gave her a smile. "Hi. Tell me you have beer."

She stole a quick kiss. "I have beer. Come on in and sit. I'll grab you one."

Charlotte put the food on the kitchen counter along with that journal she carried around, which had grown stuffed with paper. "Okay. I have free hands now. I can get my own beer. You should sit." Char stepped up close and took another, longer kiss. "Your poor arm. Tell me what happened? Deenie said there was an ambulance and everything."

"Oh, I got the saw caught and just wrenched it out bad.

Someone knocked me over in the line at urgent care and I fell, so they overreacted." That wasn't exactly it, but it was close-ish.

Charlotte squinted at her, a knowing grin pulling at the corner of her lips. "Uh-huh. Nothing in there says ambulance to me, but I'll let you get away with it if you kiss me again."

"Perfect answer." She kissed Char hard this time, cupping her head in that one good hand.

Charlotte leaned right in, fingers curling in her sweatshirt. "Mmm," Charlotte hummed as they broke off. "You don't kiss like you're broken."

"I'm not. I was separating a little bit, and they shoved it back in." She winked over, going to keep the playful tone going.

Charlotte chuckled, giving her that flirty smile she liked so much. "So, this is how it's going to be is it? I'm going to spend every day worrying about you ending up in the ER."

"No, only days where I separated my shoulder because of a weird-ass chainsaw accident. I want to hear about your day. Your boss called you?" She knew that Charlotte had quit, but she was fuzzy on the details.

"Oh. No, no." Char took a beer out of the fridge. "She didn't call. She showed up at my house. At my *house*! Can you believe that?"

"No. What? No. Shit. Sit. Tell me everything. Seriously. Did you snarl?" She missed all the good stuff.

"She called me errant. *Errant*! In fucking air quotes!" Her girl was radiantly indignant. "And I just...told her what was what and threw her out." Charlotte took a huge swig of her beer and held out one finger in a "wait" gesture while she swallowed. "And the best part? Fern showed up right then like a bright and sparkly angel who'd swallowed a soccer ball and applauded me."

"Oh dude! Good for her. So did she even apologize? And wait. Errant? Excuse me?" Charlotte was a blisteringly hot, amazing, brilliant adult. Not a child.

"Errant," Char made air quotes with her fingers. "Just like that. And I didn't really give her a chance to apologize. I don't even want one. I told her I quit, opened the door, and off she went." Charlotte shook her head. "And then had a little panic, but Fern and Aunt Deenie handled it well."

"Oh, good for them! Seriously." She had to admit, she might have had to bite the lady. With an axe.

"I'm starving." Charlotte started unpacking food. "Okay so, I'm now unemployed and living with my parents in my childhood bedroom. How sexy is that?"

"You're a freelancer who can spend the night at her girlfriend's house at will. I like it."

Charlotte nodded thoughtfully. "That sounds better, but the 'at will' thing hasn't been working out so well for us."

"Not yet. I don't know about you, but post-Christmas? My life is simpler. Like whoa." And if Charlotte got bored, she'd help with that.

"Hell, when this bazaar is over I have nothing to do at all." Char winked at her. "I'll be pretty available. *Like whoa.* Taco?"

"Yes, please." Lars would bet her very busy lover would have more to do than she thought. There wasn't a lot of folks around here that did advertising, and a ton of tourist-driven businesses to help.

They spread out the food. "Good thing tacos are one-handed." Charlotte held hers up and then took a bite. "Mmm."

"Thank you for supper." The tacos were spicy and crispy and rich. So yummy. "Seriously."

"You're welcome. I needed some comfort food. So for real, baby. How much pain are you in?"

She sighed softly. "It's not too bad if I don't move. If I try to move it, it's fairly sharp. It was a stupid accident, you know? I hit a knot in the trunk."

"Then I guess you better not move it. I'll just have to pamper you tonight and do everything." Charlotte's grin made it seem like it wouldn't be much of a chore.

Oh, Char was going to spend the night. Excellent. "I'll be happy to be with you."

"Good. Oh! Oh my god, so Santa broke his leg." Char talked as she chewed. "Aaron called, and he was so apologetic that I had to be nice, right? Thank god for Fern. She found someone. They have a Great Dane we're going to make Rudolph."

"Lucy Andrew's beast? She's sweet as pie." And Bubbles was the size of a horse and loved to dress up and be praised. "Just keep telling her she's pretty, and she'll wear the antlers all damn day."

"Yes, that's the one. Are you ready for the tree lighting? Once that's done the bazaar is rolling. I can hardly believe it; it's been a haul to get here."

"I am." She'd never missed one, not in her entire life, and she sure wasn't missing this one. "I can't wait for Cheyenne DeLongh's brownies. She has peppermint ones for the bazaar. And Jenny May is excited about being able to do the live carving. Chainsaws ho!"

"No chainsaws for you yet, young lady. Oh, but I want those brownies. Yum."

"Yeah. I'm not even telling Miz Studly and Armed with a

Saw about my shoulder." Jenny could make things with her saws that were mind-blowing. Hell, there was a Santa bear and the bears at the bottom of the deck that were her work.

"She might notice the sling." Char winked at her. "I'm just glad they're all showing up. We have so many booths this year. We added about twenty, and the stage is going to be busy all day instead of just an hour or so here and there."

"Rock on. This town isn't going to know what hit it." She couldn't wait. She hadn't had much to do with it, but she was damn proud of Charlotte.

"Fern jokes that we're putting Mom out of business. The sad thing is that I think Mom is glad."

"Oh, she's got a lot on her plate right now, huh?" And the rumor mill was that she wanted to get a job at the yarn store, teaching knitting and selling overpriced string.

"I guess, with Dad and...being nosey and all." Lars got a sideways glance and then Char cracked up. "It's exhausting putting your nose in everyone else's business."

"Like I'd know. I don't get into town enough for that." Although lots of her buddies did. Lots of them.

"Mhm. You don't need to; you have a gaggle of teenagers working for you that tell you everything. I know who Vicky's mother is."

Lars let her eyes go wide. That woman was the equivalent of an old-timey telephone switchboard operator. "Right? Damn Sam."

Char's grin turned into an adorable frown. "Do you need help with your dinner, baby? You're not eating much."

"Oh, I was just talking and listening to you." She shrugged, or tried to, and her shoulder reminded her just how shitty an idea that was.

"Hurts, huh? Do you have something to help you sleep?"

"I've got a heating pad and some pain pills. They make me queasy, though." She wrinkled her nose. She hated feeling out of control and blah.

"That sucks. You need sleep." Charlotte tapped her hand. "Food will help with the meds."

"Sorry. Sorry. They are good. Can you get me a paper plate and a fork, honey? Please?"

"Yes. All you had to do was ask. You're still a stud, you know." Char brought her what she needed. "I mean, how many people get to say their girlfriend got into a fight with a fucking chainsaw and won?"

"A fucking chainsaw is probably the name of a wild vibrator…"

"I think that would be out of my league." Char rolled her eyes. "I'll google it. After you eat. Can I stay over? Or are you the stoic in public type that wants to be alone?"

"I'd love for you to stay. Please." In fact, Charlotte could just stay for the duration, however long that was.

"Good. Yay. I'd planned to and then… I don't know, I suddenly doubted myself. I guess I should have known better; even Goober isn't treating me like a guest anymore."

"You aren't a guest. You're my lover. You belong. I need to get you a key."

"A key? For real? Like a come over whenever I want key? Or as in case you have another fight with a chainsaw and lose your key in the snow key?"

"Yes. And yes, yes, yes, and yes." Hopefully that was all the questions. If not, she'd try again.

Charlotte stared at her a second, then started to laugh. "So the extra yes was about whether I should just basically, like, move in, right?"

"Absolutely. Totally. You know I want you." And she was completely sure of that.

"I know, but are you sure you want my vortex of chaos in your home?" Char winked at her.

"You like my dogs, you like my spaghetti sauce, and you look amazing in my bed. Then there's the whole love bit, so... Yeah." She didn't stress it at all, really.

"The love bit is kind of a thing, yeah." Char kissed her cheek. "It's a big thing." Char sipped her beer while she finished her taco with a fork.

"It is. It's huge." She found herself just watching Charlotte. Her lady was beautiful. Stunning.

"Okay, you. You're looking kind of pale. I think it's time to tuck you in, baby." Char set her beer down and started cleaning up. "Does Goob need to go out?"

"Yeah, please." She had the doggie door, but she had him go out and shut the door before bed because foxes.

Raccoons.

Porcupines.

Baby bears.

"Okay. You haul your super-hot butt upstairs. I'll take care of Goob and the kitchen."

"Hey." She stood and gave Char a gentle kiss. "I'm proud of you."

It had to take a lot to quit your job, tell off your boss, in front of your family.

Charlotte's face bloomed into a smile in stages—first curious, then a shy smile and a pretty blush, then a full-on pleased grin. "Yeah? No one really ever told me that before. Out loud like that. Besides Fern. Thank you."

"I thought you should know." Okay, she'd done good. It felt so good, she'd try to do it again. "I'll meet you upstairs."

"Be careful, baby. I'll be up soon."

Lars hauled her ass up the stairs, brushed her teeth, and toed off her shoes before she snuggled in the sheets.

She had her girl, her pup, and a full belly. It wasn't perfect, but it was close.

17

S o.
Many.

People.

Charlotte stood in the center of the Cedar Ranch event barn just watching and being jostled by shoppers as they dodged and weaved and made their way through the bazaar crowds. It was hard to believe that this was only about half of the vendors. Folks that needed more space had booths outside, lining both sides of the barn.

Christmas music played inside, and all the bands and other live acts played on the outdoor stage.

It was loud, it was busy, and today was only half over.

It was a success is what it was, and Charlotte didn't want to jinx anything, but she could feel that pride all the way to her pinky toes.

Even if they'd had a belly dancing version of the Nutcracker, a heavy metal band doing The "Carol of the Bells", and there was a psychic tent with jingle bells on it in the back...

And every so often that chainsaw would go off, carving into another stump of wood, drowning everything out.

But normally they got all the locals and old-timers and craft people. That heavy metal band brought the teenagers. And the belly dancing? Fern had put flyers up the resort at Pine Valley.

Fucking genius.

Santa and Woofdolph the Great Reindane were a hit, Cheyenne DeLongh's booth had had a line ten deep all day, and Mom was in charge of the craft barn.

If she could convince Naomi to stop giving sled rides to kids, it would be great.

Who was she kidding? Naomi's shoulder was healed enough that she could function without the sling, and she hadn't smiled like that all week. She was loving those kids.

Charlotte wiggled her way out of the barn and into the fresh air. The weather couldn't have been better—chilly but sunny, snowy mountain views right up to the open blue sky.

There were men pulling the ropes to haul sledders up the hill, seven ice carvings, thirty-five snowmen, and at least a dozen fully themed, decorated Christmas trees up for auction.

The North Pole had exploded over the farm.

"All these booths and I can't find the damn hot chocolate."

"Fern!" Charlotte grinned at her friend. "Whoa. Did you grow?"

"I don't know. I feel like a whale that's swallowed the moon."

That looked about right. "Let's get you that hot chocolate and a chair. Can you believe all of this? We're amazing!"

"We are. This has been the most fun! And, guess what?" Fern's cheeks were bright red, almost glowing. "I talked to

Troy, and he's not reupping. He says it's time to come home. Like home."

"Oh, Fern, that's great!" She gave Fern a careful hug and chuckled. "So he'll be home for number three?"

"We'll be here. Mom and Dad are buying one of the new condos right on the edge of town, so we're buying their house!"

"What? No way!" She leaned in closer. "I'm moving too. There's this farm up the road with all these dogs…"

"No shit!" That came out really loud, and Fern clapped her hand over her mouth, looking around for little Alicia, even though they both knew she was in with Fern's mom and Aunt Deenie, working at the cookie exchange. "For real? We're going to be able to see each other for coffee and spa days and lunch?"

"Yes! Coffee and shopping and…next year's bazaar? I'll babysit." She needed Fern's help; this thing had a mind of its own now.

"Yes. Of course yes. You're going to be blissfully happy with your lumberjack and the dogs, and I'll have two children to remind you don't have to have babies!"

"My lumberjack." She laughed and took Fern's arm. God, she loved Fern. Fern just got it. Fern had always gotten it. "Hot chocolate. Right there. You want to sit? I'll bring you some."

"I do, honey. My back is killing me." Fern rubbed her back, a little frown between her eyebrows. "I am carrying a bowling ball, though."

"You sure are. One of those orange swirly ones. Sit, you. I'll be right back." Man, Fern looked ready to pop. She remembered this with Alicia; Fern had waddled around all frowny and uncomfortable for days.

She grinned as she shook her head. She was never doing

this to herself. Fern was probably going to have six or eight and she would never need to. She waited in line a few minutes to order. The place was that popular. "Two hot chocolates please, extra whipped cream." Ooh. Maybe they needed a skating rink next year...

"You got it! How's it going, boss lady?" She got a huge grin and a wink.

"Good! Really good. I just need to sit for a minute. Business seems good, right?"

"It's amazing. This is—you've breathed new life into this. You ought to see if you can do the planning for the Wine, Whitewater, and Whimsy Fest in the summer! I know Dave Marker stepped down."

"Did he?" Well, that was interesting. That planning would need to start right after this one ended. "I'll...see what I can find out. Thanks. Happy sales!" She grabbed the drinks and went back to Fern.

"Oh, that smells good. What's wrong? You look... thoughtful." Fern took one of the cups from her.

"Not wrong...intriguing." She sat slowly and leaned back in her chair. "Dave Marker isn't doing the summer Whimsy festival thing anymore."

"No?" Fern gave her a quick glance. "I don't suppose a festival-wedding-party planning partnership is on your list of neat ideas to try with a friend?"

She grinned at Fern. "Oh, it's at the top of my list. The very, very tippy fucking top. Fern! We would rock that." A plan. Holy shit a plan just fell in her lap. With Fern. Holy fucking shit.

Fern held out her hand. "Well then, partner...let's rock this."

"I can't wait to tell Naomi." She looked around like

mentioning her love's name would make her appear. "She's going to love it."

"We'll have to have supper or something tonight, so I can get to know her—" Fern tensed suddenly, her eyes going wide.

"What? What's...there's a bear behind me?" She turned and looked over her shoulder not sure what she was expecting to see, but there was nothing there. "Fern, what are—Fern?" Uh-oh.

"Uh-huh." There was a puddle forming under Fern. "I need to call Troy."

"Okay. You call. I'll get a car." Oh fuck. *Fuck.* She glanced around looking for a familiar face but didn't see one. No problem, she refused to panic, Fern deserved better. "You breathe, okay? And stay right here."

"Right. My mom's got Alicia."

Charlotte texted as she ran, and like magic, Naomi appeared. "Hey, love. What's up?"

"Fern's water broke, and we're having a baby!" She kept running, letting Naomi follow. She was on a mission. "Need wheels."

"You need my truck? I got my keys."

"Is it close?" She stopped and stared at Naomi. "Oh my god, I can't leave the bazaar can I? Maybe you should go with her."

"Me? I—Sure. Of course. Vicky's got the dogs. Where's her mom?"

"I'll call her mom. You're the best. She needs to get to the hospital. No clinic, okay?" She kissed Naomi's cheek. "I just need to get my Mom and Jacob to cover me, and I'll be there as soon as I can. You can call me if things get...you know, baby like."

"Baby like. I'll text Vicky about the dogs. I need to make sure they're taken care of, okay?"

"I promise. Jacob loves dogs."

Naomi nodded and followed her to Fern, who was looking wide-eyed around the edges.

"Charl—I got to go."

"You're coming with me. You won't hurt the seats in my truck." Naomi winked at Fern. "I'll get you to the hospital and stay with you, okay?"

"And I'll be there as soon as I get Mom and Aunt Deenie and Jacob on board to cover me here. I promise." She helped Fern up. "Plus, Naomi drives like a bat out of hell."

"I so do. Hell, we could take the sled, if you want." Naomi winked at Fern, moving them toward the parking lot.

"Right? I'd heard you like...oh, whoa..." Fern stopped walking a second and took a deep breath. "Like to rescue women with that sled." Fern started walking again.

Charlotte exchanged a worried look with Naomi behind Fern's back.

"I saw that you two. This isn't my first rodeo. I've got this. Just get me to the church on time, lumberjack."

"I can do that. I'm parked over here. Thank goodness I unhitched the trailer."

They got Fern into the truck and belted in. "I'll make absolutely sure that Vicky's got the dogs and can feed Goober. Thank you, baby. I just can't run off and leave this. I'll... I need an hour? Two at most and then I'll be on my way."

"I'm on this. See you soon." Naomi winked at her, and hopped in the truck, spinning out of the parking lot like she had a woman in labor in the truck.

Charlotte watched them disappear and then took a deep

breath and shook out her hands, trying to let the minor panic go.

Okay. She needed to find Vicky, then Mom.

Fast.

She had another goddaughter on the way.

18

"So, baby number two, eh? How long were you in labor with number one?" Dogs took forever sometimes, she knew.

"Six hours, and I've been cramping for about a day. I just wanted to get through the bazaar."

Lars stepped on the gas. Fuck a duck. "Well, cross your legs, woman, and call your husband."

"He's hard to reach. You didn't have to do this, I appreciate it." Fern was clearly uncomfortable, but she was handling it like a champ. Her hands weren't even shaking as she dialed, and dialed again, trying to get through to someone.

"I won't leave you in the lurch." Charlotte would kill her, and she'd just managed to convince her to stick around.

"I know. Charlotte trusts you, so I do. She's a tough one to impress."

"She's amazing. She cares about you a ton. Are you having a boy or a girl, do you know?"

"It's another girl. Poor Troy is going to be even more

outnumbered." Fern shifted in her seat. "He's coming home after this tour. He's out."

"Are you excited? Are you staying where you're posted?" La la la, talking to the woman in labor, keeping things calm.

"Oh, no. Well, I'm staying—whoo boy—" Fern took a breath and puffed it out. "That was fun. I'm staying with Mom and Dad right now, but they're going to buy one of the fancy new condos at the edge of town, and Troy and I are buying their...place."

"Yeah? How cool is that? What does he want to do?" *Don't you have a baby in my truck.*

"He hasn't said yet, but he's handy. His dad builds h—houses, his brother does roofing. He might...whoo..." There was a longer pause this time. "He might want to go to college? I don't know."

"I go online, believe it or not. We've got fifteen minutes. Squeeze."

"Uh-huh. Squeezing." Fern chuckled weakly but stopped abruptly. "Oh, that was a bad idea. So...online, huh? That's an idea."

"Yeah. People respect them, you can do it online, and it's cheaper."

"That would be great. I might ask more when I'm not trying to not have a baby." Fern grinned at her. "They're not super close together, just...strong."

"Cool." She thought. Maybe. "What does that mean?"

"Obviously that you're not going to be the one to convince Charlotte to have babies."

Oh, for chrissake. "Yeah...no."

Fern chuckled carefully. "She hasn't ever wanted to be a mother. Not in as long as I've known her. I think it's one of the reasons the bitch fiancée left her. She didn't believe Char was serious. And Charlotte is very serious."

"I hire a lot of teenagers, but I'm not interested in raising little ones. Dogs are enough for me."

"Well you and Charlotte will see plenty of mine now." Fern pointed out the window. "Hospital! Oh, thank god. Thank you. I'm here." Fern's phone rang and she tapped it four or five times in a row before it finally answered. "Babe? Yes, it's time. I feel good. I just got to the—I'm fine. I'm here, yes. She's with Mom."

Lars let that conversation go on and tried not to eavesdrop too much as she pulled into the parking lot and up to the emergency room door.

"I gotta go, babe. I'm at the ER. Everything is good. I'll have Charlotte keep you up to date. Yes. I love you! Love you. Bye." Fern sighed and hung up, then swiped tears from her face. "Well, here I go without him again."

"For the last time, right? He'll be home to stay." She hopped out and grabbed a wheelchair. "I'll get you in, move the car, and then come in to stay with you."

Fern nodded, for the first time showing some signs of cracking around the edges. But by the time Lars got back with the wheelchair, that was gone, and Fern was cheerfully making whale song as Lars and a broad-shouldered male nurse hauled her down from the passenger seat and into the wheelchair.

"Back. Sorry. Charlotte texted that she'll pick up your bag, and that your momma has your little girl." And she'd said not to panic.

Right.

No panicking.

"Good. Great. Thank yo—ooh. Wow. This little girl means business."

"No babies in the ER!" The nurse, whose badge read

"Brady", chuckled and took off with the wheelchair. "We'll just get you right to maternity and check you in up there."

"Works for me!"

"Are you the other momma?" Brady asked as they got on the elevator.

"I am most certainly not. I'm the girlfriend of the best friend."

"The—wow."

"I know. I'm the pinch-hitter." And she thought Charlotte had better hurry.

"She's amazing." Fern groaned and shifted in her chair.

Brady shook his head. "I don't know, you might be up to bat, best friend's girlfriend."

Goodie. "I'm right here. It's not like you guys need me to catch it."

"Or that you've never seen girl parts before." Fern was panting now.

"True that. Is this goddamn elevator not moving?"

Brady laughed, and a second later the elevator chimed. "Third floor, lingerie!"

"Don't make me laugh, man." Fern chuckled anyway. "Oh god, will I ever be able to wear lingerie again?"

"Not as long as you keep getting knocked up, Momma." Lars tried not to laugh. Honest she did.

"Ha! Didn't I just tell you Troy is coming home for... goddammit, Brady get me out of this chair!"

"Yes, ma'am. Hold on there." Brady had already made eye contact with another nurse who took off down the hall to get a room ready. "Can you just wait out here for a few minutes, and we'll call you in?"

"Totally! No problem!" As soon as Fern disappeared into the room, she called Charlotte. "Babe, that baby is coming. Imminently. Like whoosh."

"No, really? Shit. I'm driving. I'll be there soon. Is she okay? Is she swearing yet? Is she crowning? How far apart are her contractions?"

"How many of those words am I supposed to understand, exactly?" Crowning? What the actual fuck?

"Naomi." Charlotte laughed. "Okay. Are you with her? Just hold her hand and tell her she's a rock star. That's it. Can you do that?"

"Totally." The door opened, and the nurse waved her in, looking a little frantic. "Gotta go. Love you. Bye!"

Fern was crying, and there was some horrible shit happening down south, so Lars grabbed Fern's hand and held on. "You are a goddamn rock star, woman."

CHARLOTTE LOOKED at her keys as she paced in the elevator wondering if she'd locked the truck. And where she parked it.

Hopefully she'd turned the headlights off.

Was this elevator even moving? "Come on, come on."

She hadn't taken the time to call and say she was here; it wasn't not like Fern could slow down and wait for her.

She stepped right up to the doors as the floor chimed and ran for the nurse's desk.

"Fern Gonzalez? I'm her best friend. I'm late. Or...she's like two weeks early but you know what I mean."

"Five-thirty-four." The nurse pointed and started to say something else, but Charlotte didn't stop to listen. She just barreled through the door.

"Fern?"

Naomi stood there, wide-eyed, while Fern cradled her newest little girl. Oh. Oh, dear.

"Oh my god. I missed it." She hurried to Fern and smiled at the new baby. "Hey, little girl. You just couldn't wait for me, huh?"

"She didn't. She was on a mission." Fern chuckled. "Lars is in charge of taking pictures for Troy."

Her poor Naomi didn't look like she wanted to be in charge of anything right now. "Oh. Did you get him on the phone yet? Let me get him on the phone." She dragged Fern's phone off the little rolling tray table next to the bed.

"Not yet. Lars cut the cord for me. I told her she gets to be the co-godmother with you, since she didn't even gag during the whole process."

Oh boy. "Impressive. Sounds like she earned it." She glanced at Naomi and did not laugh. She didn't even let herself grin at the traumatized look on Naomi's face. "She's beautiful, Fern. You did good, lady." She looked back at Fern's phone and dialed Troy.

"Hey, baby!"

"Nope. Charlotte. You have a little girl." She handed Fern the phone, and Naomi gave her a grin.

"So, that was exciting. How did the end of the bazaar go?"

"I don't know, it goes until eight. We'll have to ask Jacob or Mom later. But it was going well when I left." She slipped her arms around Naomi's waist, grinning at her. "Cut the cord, huh? You look a little...wigged, baby."

"Do I? It was cool. She rocked it, and that little baby was *mad*." Naomi shook her head. "And tiny? Jesus, honey. She's just wee bitty."

"Yeah, that's wild isn't it? She's two weeks early...maybe a tiny bit more. She was definitely not expected just yet. You'd be pissed off too if you were all warm and cozy and got shoved out into this looney bin."

"Right. I was probably hatched from an egg."

"My Dino-lumberjack." She kissed Naomi gently. "Thank you for doing this. Being here. She's...it's hard not having Troy here."

"Hey." Naomi caught her gaze. "She's your best friend. She's going to be part of my extended family too, right?"

"She already is, god-mom." She couldn't imagine anyone —literally anyone else she'd ever dated—doing this for her, for Fern. "Family. I like that."

"You know it. What do we do now? I'm sort of out of my league."

"Whatever she wants. We fuss over the baby and tell Fern how pretty she is until her mom gets here and then we're off the hook tonight. I'll be on call for a day or two until she leaves the hospital, and then for a couple of weeks to get Alicia out of her hair or bring ice cream or just keep her company. She said Troy was coming home, but I'm not sure if that means weeks or months."

She glanced over at Fern who was FaceTiming with Troy, showing him the baby.

"Oh! Did she name her yet?"

"Not that I know of, no. There were just the prerequisite tears and stuff." Naomi chucked and shook her head. "Tell me again that we aren't going to have to do this."

She squinted at Naomi. "There is no way in hell I'm popping one of those out. And better? We can't have an oopsie. Wanna spit-shake on it?"

"Nah. I've seen enough bodily fluids today. I want to go have a huge steak and a hot fudge sundae the size of my head."

She giggled. That was the best idea ever. "And mashed potatoes. You're on. First, when she hangs up with Troy, we fuss and tell her how pretty the baby is. Got it?"

"Totally. She looks like a bright red old man, but she has all her fingers and toes." Naomi gave her a serious look. "Don't worry. Newborn puppies are ugly too, and look how they turn out."

Charlotte kissed her quickly, because Naomi totally got it and not everyone did. "You're amazing, have I told you that lately?"

"Yeah, but you can tell me again. I earned it today."

"Here's a bonus. You're amazing and I love you."

Naomi's smile beamed at her like sunshine. "I'm going to step out, call Vicky, and check on the dogs, give you a chance to talk to Fern."

Something about making Naomi smile like that made her feel like Superwoman. "Okay, baby. We'll be done here soon." Char squeezed her hand.

Naomi slipped out the door about the time Fern hung up with Troy. Fern was crying softly, and Charlotte went to sit and hold Fern's hand.

"You're okay."

"No, but he's coming home soon. He says four weeks. Then he'll go pack up the house in one of those pod-things, and he'll be here. He says just stay."

"What about all your baby stuff that's at the house?" Fern would need some of that in the next month, surely.

"I don't know. I'll figure it out. Tomorrow."

"Tomorrow is good. Remember, I have a truck, a lumberjack, and no job." She winked at Fern. "All I need is a key to your house."

"Right! And she won't be busy after Christmas. You two could have a road trip to San Fran!" Fern nuzzled the top of her baby's head. "Besides, Jenna and Alicia and I know you need to empty your apartment in Denver, too."

"Jenna. That's pretty, I like it." And a road trip to San

Francisco sounded fabulous actually. As long as Naomi could get the dogs looked after they'd been good. "I can't believe I missed her delivery. But it seems like it all went well. Did you give Naomi hell?"

"She was great. She teased and joked and was here. She's not you, but I love that she was willing to show up." Fern searched her eyes. "And I can tell, she's really in love with you."

She blushed because she knew it was true, and then she blushed more because blushing was embarrassing, and then she just gave up and rolled her eyes. "Yeah. I think so. And the feeling is mutual. I'm sorry I wasn't here, though. I had to find some folks to look after *our* baby."

"Yes. Yeah. I swear, once I get a few days to settle, I'm on this, Lottie."

"Nonsense." They weren't in that big of a hurry. "We'll make a plan to present after the New Year." Good grief, she wasn't going to ask Fern to do anything for a bit. New baby, new house, holidays, Troy coming home... Fern had enough on her plate. "Right now, you get to be Mommy."

"I do. You want to hold her?" Fern was smiling and crying at the same time.

"Yes. Can I?" She let Fern have her tears. She understood them, and if she wandered off with the baby for a second it would give Fern a chance to breathe. "I forgot how tiny newborns are. She seems smaller than Alicia was." Alicia had been a chunker. She took Jenna carefully.

"She is. Almost three pounds lighter. She looks like Troy. She's perfect. I can't wait for Alicia to meet her."

"She is perfect. Are you hungry? Do you need a Coke or anything?" She shuffled around the room, watching Jenna sleep and giving Fern a little space.

"Not to eat, but a Coke would be welcome. Something

with bubbles?" Fern grinned at her, suddenly slumping in the sheets. "I had a baby, Lottie, with your lumberjack holding my hand and smelling like dogs."

"You had a baby. This one right here. Congratulations. And if she wasn't already, Naomi is definitely family now, huh?" She placed little Jenna back in Fern's arms.

"Yes." Fern shot her half a smile, but her focus was on little Jenna.

"I heard I'm a grandmother." Janet came in slowly and speaking quietly. This was a woman that understood infants. "Hello, Lottie." She got a quick hug, and then Fern's mother turned her attention to her family.

She laid a hand on Fern's arm. "I'll get that Coke," she whispered, and left the room, finding Naomi outside waiting for her. "I promised the new mom a Coke."

"Ah, they're over here." Naomi got her a Coke and a cup of ice. "Ta-da!"

That smile on Naomi's face wasn't fading, and that totally did it for her. "Resourceful too. I think I'll keep you around. Give me two seconds and then I'm going to get you that steak."

When she popped back into the room, Janet was holding the baby, and Fern was napping. "Looks like you have everything under control," she said softly, and set the Coke down for Fern to have later.

"I think we're fine, honey. Go get some rest. Come by in the morning so I can go shopping." Janet definitely looked like she was in her happy place.

"Will do. Congratulations."

Charlotte slid a hand into Naomi's as soon as she left the room. "Ready?"

"God yes. Let's go, honey. I earned that steak."

Charlotte hustled Naomi onto the elevator. "See? This is

perfect. We got to play aunties and now, we get to go have grownup steaks and not change any diapers at two in the morning."

"Oh, I do like this part. You're a smart broad." Naomi goosed her.

She smacked Naomi's hand away playfully. "Oh, and we're taking a trip to San Francisco after the holidays."

"Are we? Cool. I'm so in. I've never been."

Not why? Not when? Just I'm so in.

"Yeah? Me either." And that was that. "It'll be another adventure."

"One of many, honey. One of many."

EPILOGUE

Epilogue

"Oh Jesus, baby! That one went down my back!" Charlotte squirmed in her parka, trying to escape the frozen snowball that was slowly melting against her skin. She scooped up a double handful of snow and stalked Naomi. It wasn't like they weren't both already covered in snow from their amazing dogsled ride, but she wasn't going down easy.

Naomi looked radiant in the Christmas morning sun—her cheeks were pink from the wind and her smile bright as the day. But beautiful or not, they were rivals at the moment, hurling snowballs as they ran back to the house to warm up. "You're so dead."

"Listen to you! Be careful, you might break a nail!"

When she stopped to snarl, Naomi pegged her right in the chest, eyes dancing.

"That's cheating! I had them painted candy cane striped just for the holidays." She tossed her head, playing offended, and when her girl came in to sweep the snow off her chest, she pulled back Naomi's hood and stuffed a snowball into Naomi's parka.

Then she ran for the front door.

Naomi caught her at the door, gloves flying just before icy hands slid into her snow pants. Oh, that really was cheating!

"Cold! No. Nope!" She wiggled, dragging her gloves off and pummeling Naomi with them, snow flying. "Stop! Oh my god."

Naomi cupped her, dragging her close. "Ho ho ho?"

She gasped, still half-laughing, not sure if she was breathless from the cold or the touch. "I...sure, okay. Ho it is..."

Naomi cracked up, hugging her tight before letting her go. "Coffee or cocoa, o' Queen of the Christmas Bazaar."

"More like Queen of the Bizarre, but here we are." She gave Naomi her best flirty smile. "A mocha, please. With whipped cream. Is that too high maintenance?"

"For you, pretty lady, never." Naomi leaned down, kissed her hard enough she saw snowflakes. "Welcome home."

Interested in learning more about BA's cowboys and Jodi's gentlemen? Want free fiction and news? Join our newsletters!

What's Up with Jodi
https://readerlinks.com/l/2317334

Spurs and Shifters
https://lp.constantcontact.com/su/A9CRUzp/baandjulia

BA & JODI'S SUMMIT SPRINGS NOVELS

Tipping the Barrel
By BA Tortuga

Cowgirl Evie Martin has her ranch, her horses, a bunch of goats, and a million side hustles to make ends meet. So if she misses the one who got away, well, who has time for romance and relationships? At least that's what she tells herself until that one special woman comes back into her life, needing her help.

Barrel racer Cheyenne DeLongh was rodeo royalty until an accident took her best horse and left her with scars that are both visible and deep-hidden. The only place she can think to go is to the woman she still loves. Evie. If her mother could stop meddling and Evie can believe that Cheyenne wants to stay and be a small town rancher, she might just get her stuff together. But as much as Evie loves Cheyenne, can she ever believe she'll be enough to make Cheyenne stay?

Tipping the Barrel is a cowgirl romance with meddling family, second chances, a small town setting, and a happy ending.

Read More Here

Top of the World
by Jodi Payne

She could have found a job anywhere, but Frankie chose Summit Springs for a reason. Her name is Aspen Young.

Frankie Hoffman is excited about her new job in Summit Springs, developing a mountain biking adventure program for M&M Outfitters. Riding is her passion, and she loves every adrenaline fueled moment of her sport. Sure, she could have gotten a similar seasonal job back in Vermont, but Frankie chose Summit Springs for a reason, and her name is Aspen Young.

Aspen is a potter who moved home to Summit Springs to pursue her dream of owning an art gallery. Keeping the gallery's doors open and her co-op of resident artists in business keeps her busy enough that she never thinks about Frankie anymore, and she has completely buried her broken heart.

Aspen's not impressed when she comes home to find Frankie standing in her kitchen, and she doesn't mince words when it's time for Frankie to go home, making it clear she doesn't want to see her ex again. But Frankie came a long way to win Aspen back and one rejection isn't going to shake her resolve. Can she make amends and get through Aspen's walls?

Top of the World is a second chances Sapphic (lesbian, F/F) romance set in the fictional town of Summit Springs, Colorado, featuring an ice queen artist and her mountain biker, rough and tumble ex.

Read More Here

WANT MORE SUMMIT SPRINGS BOOKS?

Check out the other books in the series!

Happy Holidays, Y'all!

We want to thank you for giving Christmas Bizarre a try. We hope you enjoyed the story.

If you can spare a few minutes to post a review at the retail website where you made your purchase, we'd very much appreciate it!

Don't forget to "like" our Facebook pages and groups to keep up with all the news--new releases, sales announcements, giveaways, sneak peeks-- and of course the rodeo pictures, coffee memes and just general fun. We'd love to have all y'all!

Yeehaw and thanks for reading!

BA & Jodi

ABOUT JODI

JODI takes herself way too seriously and has been known to randomly break out in song. Her men are imperfect but genuine, stubborn but likable, often kinky, and frequently their own worst enemies. They are characters you can't help but fall in love with while they stumble along the path to their happily ever after. For those looking to get on her good side, Jodi's addictions include nonfat lattes, Malbec and tequila any way you pour it.

Website: jodipayne.net
Newsletter: https://readerlinks.com/l/2317334
All Jodi's Social Links: linktr.ee/jodipayne

ABOUT BA

Texan to the bone and an unrepentant Daddy's Girl, BA Tortuga spends her days with her basset hounds, getting tattooed, texting her grandbabies, and eating Mexican food. When she's not doing that, she's writing. She spends her days off watching rodeo, knitting and surfing Pinterest in the name of research. BA's personal saviors include her wife, Julia Talbot, her best friends, and coffee. Lots of coffee. Really good coffee.

Having written everything from fist-fighting rednecks to hard-core cowboys to werewolves, BA does her damnedest to tell the stories of her heart, which was raised in Northeast Texas, but has heard the call of the high desert and lives in the Sandias. With books ranging from hard-hitting GLBT romance, to fiery ménages, to the most traditional of love stories, BA refuses to be pigeon-holed by anyone but the voices in her head.

BA loves to talk to her readers and can be found at http://batortuga.com/ and her newsletter signup link is http://bit.ly/BAJulianews

AVAILABLE FROM JODI & BA

Sapphic Romance

Christmas Bizarre, a Summit Springs

MM Romance

The Cowboy and the Dom Trilogy

First Rodeo, Book One

Razor's Edge, Book Two

No Ghosts, Book Three

The Soldier and the Angel, a Cowboy and Dom Novel

Sin Deep, a Cowboy and Dom Novel

East Meets Westerns

(single titles)

Wrecked

Flying Blind

Special Delivery, A Wrecked Holiday Novel

Temptation Ranch

Cowboy Protection

The Merry Everything Series

Cowboy Protection

Window Dressing

The Higher Elevation Series

Heart of a Cowboy

Land of Enchantment

Keeping Promises

Bigger Than Us

The Triskelion Series

Breaking the Rules

Making a Mark

Making the Rules

Les's Bar Series

Just Dex

Hide Bound

The Lone Star Series

Tending Tyler

Roped In

The Collaborations Series

Refraction

Syncopation

Puzzles Series

Cryptic

Made in the USA
Monee, IL
18 September 2023

42916187R00116